## PRAISE FOR THE JAMIE JOHNSON SERIES

"You'll read this and want to get out there and play"
Steven Gerrard

"True to the game . . . Dan knows his football"
Owen Hargreaves

"An inspiring read for all football fans"
Gary Lineker

"If you like football, this book's for you"
Frank Lampard

"Jamie could go all the way"
Jermain Defoe

"Pure class – brings the game to life"
Owen Coyle

"I love reading about football and it
doesn't get much better than this"
Joe Hart

"Pure joy"
*The Times*

"Inspiring"
*Observer*

"Gripping"
*Sunday Express*

"A resounding victory"
*Telegraph*

## ABOUT THE AUTHOR

Dan Freedman grew up wanting to be a professional footballer. That didn't happen. But he went on to become a top football journalist, personally interviewing the likes of Cristiano Ronaldo, Lionel Messi, David Beckham and Sir Alex Ferguson. He uses his passion and knowledge of football to write the hugely popular series of Jamie Johnson football novels. When he is not writing, Dan delivers talks and workshops for schools. And he still plays football whenever he can.

www.danfreedman.co.uk
www.jamiejohnson.info
Follow Dan on Twitter @DanFreedman99

# DAN FREEDMAN

final Whistle

SCHOLASTIC

First published in the UK in 2012 by Scholastic Children's Books
An imprint of Scholastic Ltd
Euston House, 24 Eversholt Street
London, NW1 1DB, UK
Registered office: Westfield Road, Southam, Warwickshire, CV47 0RA
SCHOLASTIC and associated logos are trademarks and/or registered
trademarks of Scholastic Inc.

ISBN 978 1407 11144 5

A CIP catalogue record for this book is available from the British Library

Printed and bound by CPI Group (UK) Ltd, Croydon, CR0 4YY
Papers used by Scholastic Children's Books are made from wood
grown in sustainable forests.

7 9 10 8

www.scholastic.co.uk/zone

# Acknowledgements

Thanks to:

Cecil Altman for showing what it is to be a gentleman.

Major and Phillip for all your fantastic ideas.

Caspian Dennis, Sally Rosser, Ena McNamara, Lola Cashman, Martin Hitchcock, Francine McMahon, Xabier De Beristain Humphrey, Dr Eli Silber, Gary Lewin, Michelle and Robert Farrer for your advice in writing the book.

Joe Hart, Stuart Mawhinney, Ugo Ehiogu, Alex Stone, Jim Sells, Laura Henry, Koye Sowemimo and Oli Karger for your support.

Hazel Ruscoe – this story is inspired by ideas we had together.

Ms Pluckrose, Ms Clarke, Ms Nelson, Ms Slaven and all the secret agents at St Ed's, George Heriot's, St Agnes and Nova Hreod for your brilliant feedback.

Sam and Joe Talbot, Martin Prothero and David Dein for helping to take Jamie's career to the next level.

Helen Thomas, Jessica White, Sam Perrett and the whole team at Scholastic for everything you have done for Jamie Johnson.

And to everyone who has followed Jamie's story. We've had a ball.

Part
One

# ① The Big Move

"I can't believe it!" Jamie Johnson blurted out as he burst into the hastily arranged meeting at Hawkstone United's stadium. "Is it true? Do they *really* want me?!"

Tony Walsh, the chairman of the club, Harry Armstrong, the Hawkstone manager, and Archie Fairclough, the assistant manager, were already there waiting for Jamie. As one, they nodded back at him.

This time it *was* for real. This time it was the club that Jamie wanted. Desperately.

The whole summer had been a game of transfer cat and mouse. Real Madrid, Bayern Munich and Paris St Germain had all tried to sign Jamie following his stunning performances for Scotland at the World Cup. He was one of the most sought-after players in world football.

And yet, no matter how much money they had offered to pay, Jamie had turned down each one of them. His response had always been the same: there was only one football club in the world for which he would leave Hawkstone United. But that club had never made a bid.

Until now.

Jamie's brain had been boiling with ideas since Archie had called him with the news forty-five minutes before.

This was big. This was huge.

"Barcelona want to sign *me*?!" Jamie panted. His heart was beating so fast he felt as though he'd just played four whole football matches in a row.

This was the team of teams. The club of clubs. The side who played the best football that Jamie had ever seen. And now they wanted him to join them.

"It's exciting, isn't it, Jamie?" Smiled Tony Walsh. "And a crucial decision for this club too. I think we'd prefer it if we could discuss this matter further … in private, if that's OK?"

For a second, Jamie was confused, but then he followed the line of Tony Walsh's eyes and understood he was referring to Jack, who, as ever, was right beside Jamie.

"Oh," said Jamie, catching Jack Marshall's eye with

the smile they always shared. "It's OK. Jack's cool. She may be a journalist, but you can trust her. She's my best friend. I'd tell her all this anyway, so she may as well be here now."

Tony Walsh looked at his managerial team, Harry Armstrong and Archie Fairclough, paused for a second and then, with a reluctant cough, carried on talking.

"I hope you are right, Jamie, because some of the information I am about to give you is completely confidential."

"It is true," revealed Tony Walsh as Jack and Jamie sat down. "The Barcelona delegation is flying into London as we speak. The manager, Godal, has requested a personal meeting with you tonight. They mean business, Jamie."

"You absolute beauty!" Jamie shouted, brimming with pride at the notion, his mind immediately leaping forward to imagine pulling on the famous blue and maroon top and scoring a master blaster of a shot in front of a hundred thousand adoring Barcelona fans.

It was almost every player's vision of football heaven.

"You do realize, Barcelona is the only club I would leave Hawkstone for," Jamie said, suddenly feeling a drop of sadness in his sea of ecstasy. "My granddad first brought me here when I was three. No matter what happens, Hawkstone will always be *my* club."

"We know," Walsh nodded. "In fact, you signing for Barcelona is actually the best gift you can give to Hawkstone at the moment. We need the money, Jamie. Badly."

"What do you mean?" asked Jamie. "What's the problem?"

Tony Walsh pursed his lips and looked at Harry Armstrong and Archie Fairclough. Archie, in particular, carried a troubled expression on his face.

"Look, there's no other way to say this: we're broke," stated Walsh.

"Wow," said Jamie, suddenly understanding why the Hawkstone bosses looked so serious. "But … how? I mean, we just won the league! We're doing brilliantly. Now we're going to play in the Champions League for the first time. That means we get loads of money, doesn't it?"

"We've overstretched ourselves financially, Jamie. We've been trying so hard – too hard – to get to the top and, even though we're starting to achieve some of our goals, the banks want their money back. Now."

"Right," said Jamie. "How much do we owe?"

"We need to pay fifty million pounds back to the bank before the end of August," revealed Walsh, his face growing greyer by the second.

"But that's in, like, a week!" said Jamie, panic in his voice. "What happens if we don't?"

"We go bust. They close us down. The end of Hawkstone United."

"Nine days to find fifty million?!"

"That's correct, Jamie. As a club, we've got two major playing assets. You and Bertorelli. And we've got nine days before the transfer deadline closes. We've accepted a bid for Bertorelli from Juventus this morning and now Barcelona have come in with this offer for you..."

"So, me going to Barcelona is actually a good thing for Hawkstone?" said Jamie, the images of him pulling on a Barcelona shirt once again starting to fill his mind.

Tony Walsh nodded. "The last thing any of us want is for you to leave this club. But, at this moment, that is just about the only way we have of saving it." He stroked his chin with his finger and his thumb, casting his gaze towards Jamie's knee. "The only question is, will you be able to pass a medical?"

# 2

# JOHNSON
# 11

As he and Jack walked out of the main entrance to the stadium – possibly the last time Jamie would ever do so as a Hawkstone United player – his chest brimmed with pride.

He had been brought up and played football on the streets around this ground, and now the greatest club in the world had come in to sign him.

It was perfect. Or rather, nearly perfect.

Because now Jamie had to tell the fans.

There were two hundred there already. They were being supplemented by new arrivals with each passing second as the news that Hawkstone were negotiating with Barcelona began to hit the newswires.

The fans were singing with all their might, waving

banners as they did so.

"Don't go, Jamie!"

"Hawkstone Loves You!"

Ever since the day he'd been a mascot for the club aged eleven, the Hawkstone fans had taken him to their hearts. They were so proud that a little skinny ginger kid from their streets had grown into not only one of the best players to ever pull on a Hawkstone shirt but also one of the most exciting talents in the world.

They loved Jamie and Jamie loved them.

And now he had to tell them he was leaving.

As soon as the fans saw Jamie, they rushed forward, barely able to contain themselves. These fans were pure Hawkstone. Just like Jamie.

"It's not true!" they begged.

"You're not going, are you?"

"You said all you ever wanted was to play for us in the Champions League, and now we're there you're gonna leave us!"

Jamie looked at the disappointment on the faces of the Hawkstone fans. Suddenly he felt an almost overwhelming desire to cry. He'd only ever wanted to be loved by these fans. He'd dreamed of it every time he and Jack had played football in the park. All those hours of training. All those dreams. Yet, here he was – in their eyes, at least – turning his back on them.

"It's Barcelona," was all he could muster by way of an explanation. Public speaking had never been his strength. He preferred to do his talking on the pitch. "Believe me – I would not even think about leaving Hawkstone for anyone else. But this is my chance to play for the best club in the world."

Somehow his explanation only made the fans more angry. Calling Barça the best club in the world seemed in some way to be a criticism of Hawkstone. But that was not how Jamie had meant it. He would never say a bad word about Hawkstone.

He watched a bunch of kids – all in their Hawkstone tops – as they ran off down the street, angrily kicking stray bottles and fast food containers as they went.

"Go then, Jamie!" one of them turned around and shouted.

Jamie recognized the boy; it was Robbie Simmonds. He was from the same estate as Jamie. Jamie had gone to school with his older brother, Dillon.

"You traitor!"

And with that, Robbie Simmonds tore off his Hawkstone shirt and threw it to the ground in disgust.

There was nothing Jamie could say in response. He knew that if, when he'd been younger, his favourite Hawkstone player had announced that he was leaving the club, Jamie would have reacted in exactly the same way as Robbie.

Jamie looked at Jack. They waited until the kids had turned the corner. Then, together, they walked over to where the Hawkstone top lay strewn in the street, like a dead body on a battlefield.

Jamie bent down and picked it up.

When he saw the back of the shirt, his heart sank.

He turned around and showed it to Jack, revealing the name and number on the back.

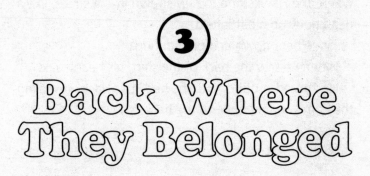

# 3
# Back Where They Belonged

"Are you a hundred per cent sure about this, Jamie?" asked Jack, spitting on her gloves and smacking her hands together as she jumped up and down on the goal-line. "You don't think it's too soon?"

Jamie didn't answer the question. Instead, he smashed the ball high up into the air. He had to do this and Jack knew it too. They had both been thinking about it during the meeting and she'd been the one who had brought it up almost as soon as they'd left the Hawkstone ground.

"But what about your knee, Jamie?" she'd asked, before the Barcelona bubble got too big and burst. "You haven't even kicked a ball since the World Cup, which, let's not forget, you came back from on crutches. How long did the docs say you should rest for if you wanted your knee to get back to normal? Six months? And that was only a month ago. Won't Barcelona be checking it out? It's got to show up in the medical, hasn't it?"

"I know," Jamie had said, each of her questions pricking his happiness like sharp needles into full balloons. "I know all of that. That's exactly why I need your help."

By "help", Jamie had meant that he needed Jack to have a kickaround with him – like in the old days. Her in goal and him smashing in the shots. He'd know in the space of five minutes whether his body, or more specifically his knee, was up to passing a medical to sign for Barcelona.

Although it had been a few years since they had played together in the park, it felt like the most natural sensation in the world for Jack and Jamie to grab a ball from Jamie's house and head down to Sunningdale Park.

This was where they had honed the skills and the passion for football that would dictate the rest of their lives – Jack as the best young female reporter in football, and Jamie as one of the world's most exciting young talents, albeit with a knee that seemed to be ageing and hurting more by the day.

He'd been advised in the strongest possible terms by the doctor for the Scotland National Team that the only way to fix his knee was complete rest. For at least six months. Only then would his injuries have time to heal. But Jamie had no time for rest. Not with Barcelona flying in tonight.

The plan was pretty simple. Jamie was going to go at this kickaround hard. Shots, sprints and skills. He needed to try out the lot. If they were all there – as good as ever – then he would know that the move to Barcelona was on. If he broke down, if his knee gave way, then the move was dead. And so was Hawkstone.

Jamie watched the ball drop from the sky. His football brain – the computer in his head – instinctively switched itself on to analyse the flight, pace and angle of the ball's descent. He arched his body backwards, offering his chest as the perfect cushion for the ball to land on.

He juggled the ball from shoulder to shoulder before letting it drop to his famous left foot. He swished his boot towards the ball, lashing it with his instep high and fast towards the top corner of the goal.

It sang through the air, arcing through the late-afternoon sun in search of its target before the topspin kicked in to provide the last-minute dip.

However, between the sticks was no ordinary goalkeeper. Jack Marshall knew Jamie Johnson, both as a person and as a footballer, better than anyone. Almost as soon as Jamie had begun his juggling routine, she'd seen the volley coming. She had started back-pedalling towards her goal a full couple of seconds before Jamie had even struck the shot. She skipped across the turf to ensure she was now in the perfect position to tip the ball nonchalantly over the crossbar with what appeared to be only the merest exertion of effort.

"Fluke!" shouted Jamie. "You only saved that 'cos you knew what I was going to do!"

"Being prepared is part of the game!" responded Jack, feeling their friendly rivalry start to reignite itself. "Anticipation's what gets you ahead in football. I always say that when I'm coaching my girls. Why? Is that the best you've got?"

Those words alone were enough to fire up Jamie's starter motor. Jack was already on her way behind the goal to collect the ball, but now Jamie was sprinting in the same direction. His pace was electric as he flew across the grass.

The wind whistled in his ears as he exploded forward. Jack turned to see Jamie coming but it was too late; he was past her in a flash, getting to the ball first and flicking it directly back over her head before running the other side of her to collect it.

Jamie stood there smiling, his foot resting on the ball. It had always been the same: him and the ball – together.

Both he and Jack knew that the pace he had just shown was not something that any normal footballer could replicate. But this boy wasn't normal. He was special. And he was ready.

"That enough to convince you I can pass the medical?" he said cheekily, even blowing Jack a mischievous kiss – such was the confidence he felt with the ball at his feet.

"Nope," responded Jack immediately. "Still need to see the overhead kick to know you're really ready... And actually, if you don't mind, I think I might film you doing it so I can show it to my team when I'm coaching them this week!"

The overhead kick had always been something unique between Jamie and Jack because, although it was now one of Jamie's trademark moves and something the Hawkstone crowd insisted he demonstrate in the warm-up before every home game, it had actually been Jack who had learned how to do it first and taught Jamie when they were eleven.

"OK! I'm filming!" announced Jack, holding her phone towards Jamie. "Right, everyone, you may well recognize the boy on the screen now. His name is Jamie Johnson. Yes, THAT Jamie Johnson, and he's very kindly agreed to show you all how to do the overhead kick. Because he's been able to do it for eight years now ... ever since a brilliant *GOALKEEPER* showed him how! OK, Jamie, remember to tell us what you're doing as you're doing it and … take it away!"

Jamie stood on the edge of the area and watched as Jack looped the ball towards him. Once again, the football computer in his brain took over, plotting the speed and path of the ball and calculating the optimum moment for him to launch himself into the air.

Then it was show time – with Jamie explaining exactly how he did it:

**1**

"As the ball comes to you, leave your kicking leg on the ground and jump into the air, leading with your other leg."

**2** "Keep your eyes on the ball. . ."

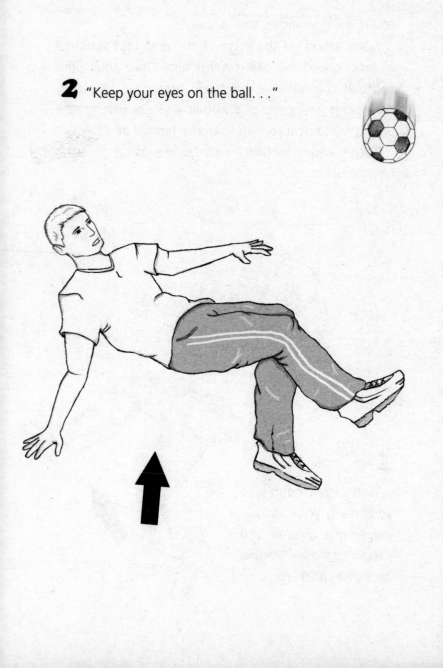

**3** "Strike the ball with your laces!"

The kids that Jack coached were lucky because it just so happened that Jamie executed what was probably one of the best overhead kicks he had ever produced. It soared with the power of a rocket right into the roof of the net. He could not have caught it any cleaner.

"Not bad," smiled Jack, saving the video and putting the phone back in her bag. "Shame Barça weren't here to see that one. They'd have signed you on the spot, even if you only had one leg... So how does it feel?"

Jamie looked down at his knee. It wasn't right. It probably never would be. He hadn't played a game of football without pain for three years. And the problem was getting worse, not better.

But Jamie knew there was enough left in the tank for him to pass this medical and sign for Barcelona.

There had to be.

# 4

# The Negotiator

"Don't panic!" said Jeremy. "I've got it all under control. Karen, where's the Spanish dictionary? And where's my comb?!"

"The car will be here in a minute, Jeremy – are you sure you don't want to sit down and have a cup of tea with me and Jamie? You're sweating quite a lot."

"Tea!" squealed Jeremy. "There's no time for TEA! And I told you not to panic! I've got it under control!"

Karen and Jamie sat on the couch and smiled as they watched Jamie's stepdad desperately wrestling with his tie as he attempted to achieve the perfect knot. Jamie could also see that Jeremy had a small bogey dangling from his left nostril. He'd leave it for a bit and tell him about it in the car. Probably.

It was certainly true that Jamie hadn't always got on with Jeremy. In fact, when his mum had first started going out with him – this boring guy she'd met working at the hospital – Jamie had thought he was a bit of a clown.

But in the last couple of years, he'd begun to understand why they were together and why they needed each other. And, compared to his dad, who had hurt Jamie more times than he could remember, at least Jamie knew one thing for certain: Jeremy would never let him or his mum down.

Jamie had told them both everything that had happened as soon as he'd got back from the park. When his mum had asked how he felt about living abroad, Jamie had simply replied that he would go to another solar system to play for Barcelona and, anyway, if he had Jack with him, he'd feel comfortable just about anywhere.

As he wasn't great with contracts and numbers, he'd asked his mum and Jeremy to go down to London with him to meet the Barcelona delegation. He'd asked Jack to come too but she had to go back to the newspaper office to write up the story of the transfer itself. This was big news.

Still, Jeremy *loved* the fact that Jamie had asked for his help. He seemed to think that Jamie wanted him to personally negotiate the terms of the contract with Barcelona and, as a result, had got himself into such a state that neither Jamie nor his mum had quite been able to calm him down.

"Right! That'll be them!" Jeremy shouted somewhat manically as the doorbell went. "I knew they'd be early. I told you there was no time for tea. This is no time for TEA! This is it. You two don't say anything. Leave everything to me! I'll do all the talking."

And with that, the three of them made their way towards the sleek black Mercedes Benz that had been sent to their home to whisk them down the motorway to London.

As they left, Jamie took a quick look around the old house that had been his home since he and his mum had needed to quickly find somewhere new to live after his dad had left them both so suddenly that dark morning twelve years before. It was a morning that had changed his life for ever.

It had been tough on his mum, he knew, bringing up a son by herself, but they had been happy enough here. The house was not big, but it had been home, and that was all that mattered.

Now, as Jamie closed the door behind them, he had an uncanny feeling that his life was, once again, about to change for ever.

# The Man From Barça

"My name is Jose Luis Armando Godal," said the coach of Barcelona Football Club, speaking perfect English as he stretched out his hand to meet Jamie's.

There had, of course, been no need for Godal to introduce himself. He was one of Jamie's biggest heroes in football.

Godal was a very short, dark-haired man who, even as a coach, looked as fit and young as any Barcelona player. He had brought a new breed of football to the club when he'd taken the helm three years prior, and the style and panache with which his team played had bewitched the entire football world.

Jamie worshipped the way Godal's Barcelona team played, and he had memorized, word for word, his post-match interview following their magical Champions League victory at the end of last season.

"I give my players three simple objectives," Godal had said that day. "Firstly, they must be the more sporting team, committing fewer fouls and being less aggressive. Then they must try to win by playing very well, more creatively than the opposition, with attacking football. And finally they need to win on the scoreboard. But we don't want to win without the first two aims being fulfilled."

For Jamie this was a new vision of the beautiful game. It wasn't just about winning football matches. It was about doing it with style.

Jamie detected the scent of aftershave as they shook hands. Godal oozed style both on and off the pitch.

"I have come to London," said the Barcelona manager, supporting his handshake with a Hollywood smile, "to sign you for the best club in the world."

Jamie almost fainted on the spot. He would have signed anything at that precise moment, such was the power of Godal's charisma.

"Er – yes, well, we will see about that, señor," said Jeremy, suddenly piping up. "We haven't agreed to anything just yet and as Jamie's ... advisor ... I am hardly going to suggest we simply accept the first offer that comes our way. You may be a very good soccer team but you are by no means the only club out ther—"

"Please," said Godal, completely unruffled by Jeremy's interjection. "Why don't you have a look at the offer first and then we can talk more?"

Godal pointed to a collection of papers that lay on the table in front of them.

"Fine," said Jeremy, taking out his glasses and flattening out the lapels of his suit jacket as he marched across the meeting room of the plush London hotel. "But, like I said, Barcelona are not the only football club in the world and I doubt very much that ... whooahhh ... hoooo ... hoooo!"

Everyone in the room stared at Jeremy as he continued to produce a series of noises that were not only completely incomprehensible but also unlike any other sounds Jamie had ever heard him make.

"He... Ho... Ha... Hooookayyyyyyy!" Jeremy finally said, fluttering the papers in front of him, producing a sound like a mad moth caught in the light. "Right, Jamie ... I think this is probably acceptable... Yes, I think I'm happy with the negotiations..."

"Jamie," said Godal, ignoring Jeremy for a second, who was now making squawking noises again as he showed Jamie's mum the contract that was on offer. "Let me talk to you alone for a second."

Godal put his reassuring arm around Jamie and

walked him to a corner of the room. "We have a saying about Barça. We say: *mes que un club*. Do you know what this means?"

Jamie shook his head.

"It means *more than a club* … and this is what Barcelona is. It is a spirit … a movement … a way of life. In our team, we have very many brilliant young players that we have trained in the Barça way of football since the age of four. And every year we search for one player from outside of Barça to come and join us. This player must have grace, glory and guts. He must be skilful, fast and brave. He must have the desire to win and, above everything else, he must share our spirit."

As Godal paused to allow Jamie to understand his words, Jamie's mind echoed the Spanish words that he had just heard.

Barcelona: *Mes que un club…*

Barcelona: More than a club…

"Jamie," smiled Godal, his voice full of certainty. "This year, we want that player to be you."

# 6
# Flying High

"It's all done and dusted," said Jamie, passing the phone from hand to hand as he got undressed for bed, talking at the same time. It was now 3.10 a.m. and he was desperate to go to sleep – but first he wanted to speak to Jack. "The contract's all signed. Jezza read every single word and he's happy – seriously happy! I'm pretty much a Barcelona player. Subject to the medical..."

"Oh ... right," said Jack, her enthusiasm suddenly punctured. "So, did they mention anything about your knee in the meeting, then? I mean, it's not exactly a secret, is it?"

"Godal just mentioned it once ... at the end," said Jamie, unconsciously running his fingers over the scars on his knee that remained from the operations that had reconstructed the joint. "He told me not to get too excited yet. Nothing's for sure until I pass the medical, but he also said that they had the best doctors in the world so, whatever happens, they'll know exactly what to do.

"They've already set the medical for three p.m. at the stadium tomorrow and told me that they're picking me up from Barcelona airport at one forty-five. That's why I'm calling, Jack... They've given me two tickets for the plane in the morning."

### Thursday 23 August

As they took their first-class seats on the plane to Barcelona, Jamie could not believe how much had happened in the twenty-four hours since the meeting at the Hawkstone ground. But with just days left until the transfer window closed, everything now needed to happen at super-speed.

"Excuse me," said Jack to one of the fellow passengers in her soft voice. "Do you think I could borrow that newspaper if you've finished with it?"

Jamie knew the man across the aisle from them stood no chance. Jack had special powers when it came to situations such as this.

"Sure!" said the man, grinning stupidly at Jack. He couldn't get the newspaper to her quickly enough. "Of course you can... Enjoy it! I mean, really, it's a cracking paper!"

Jamie laughed. The man would have surely given Jack his wallet if she had only asked.

What the man could not have known was that he was handing Jack the very article she had written only a few hours earlier. She had just accepted the job of becoming a football writer for one of the nation's bestselling newspapers, a role which she now combined with her TV work. Jack's star was rising just as quickly off the pitch as Jamie's was on it.

"Here you go," said Jack, handing Jamie the paper. They had been in such a rush to get to the airport that morning that they had barely had time to pack their passports, let alone read the papers.

"You can tell me if I've got anything wrong," she added with a typically cheeky wink.

# Football

# JOHNSON JETS OUT TO SEAL BARÇA DREAM

## Spanish giants swoop with massive bid – but move hinges on key medical

*By Jacqueline Marshall*

Only a medical examination, which will take place this afternoon, now stands between Jamie Johnson and a dream move to join Barcelona.

This comes after the Catalan giants swooped late last night to agree a fee with English champions Hawkstone United, following a summer of chasing the young winger.

With only days remaining before the transfer deadline shuts, Barcelona won the race for Johnson's signature by sending a delegation – led by manager Juan Godal – to convince Johnson that his future lay at the Nou Camp.

The deal is understood to include a large signing-on fee plus weekly wages that will dwarf anything Johnson could have expected to earn at cash-strapped Hawkstone. Meanwhile, it is also thought that Barcelona are the only team for which Johnson would have considered leaving his boyhood club.

However, this remains a deal which is far from complete. With a history of knee injuries and with Barcelona's medical examinations known for being particularly thorough, Johnson will be aware that his dream move is far from being fully sealed.

# BERTORELLI BIDS FAREWELL WITH PARTING SHOT

Matteus Bertorelli made a less than graceful exit yesterday as the exodus from Hawkstone United gathered pace. The Argentine, known as the Skilful Assassin, said of his impending move to Juventus: "Finally, I will get to live in a city with culture, sun and beautiful women. My time at Hawkstone has been like a punishment. I shall run to Turin like a lost dog returning to its master."

# NEMISAR: BARÇA HAVE MADE A MISTAKE

Fernando Nemisar, the outspoken coach of Real Madrid, has already hit out at Barcelona's proposed signing of Jamie Johnson – before he has even played a game for his new club.

When asked about Johnson's big-money move to Barcelona, Nemisar said: "We looked at this player and we could have signed him if we wanted to but I said no. He is not a player who can settle well into Spanish football.

"He is too young and he is injured too much. My doctors told me that he would never pass a medical and this is why we have let other teams make the mistake."

. . .

# JOHNSON WAS "ALWAYS DIFFERENT"

As he looked set to seal a mind-boggling switch to Barcelona, one of Jamie Johnson's oldest friends recalled the schoolboy who would one day blossom into a superstar.

"Jamie was always different to the rest," said school friend Hugo Bogson, who these days is studying to be a molecular scientist. "He always knew he was going to make it. I can still remember the day that they asked us what we wanted to be when we were older. We must have been about twelve. Of course Jamie said he was going to be a professional footballer.

"Well, what you have to remember is that Jamie was the smallest boy in our class. His birthday was late in the year and he hadn't grown up physically yet, which meant that some of the boys liked to push him about and tease him a bit. So when he said that he was going to be a footballer everyone started laughing and taking the mickey out of him.

"But Jamie wasn't laughing. He was deadly serious. Even then he had that stubborn streak of determination. When the chips were down – that's when you saw the real Jamie."

Final ticket prices

"That's mad – that piece about Boggy!" Jamie grinned. "Always wondered what happened to him! Molecular scientist! What do they do? Study moles?!"

He and Jack laughed for a second before Jamie's face went pale.

"How come you didn't put anything in about the Hawkstone fans hating me now?" he asked, handing the paper back. The sight of the kids shouting at him outside the ground yesterday still haunted Jamie. Not to mention the two eggs that someone had smashed against Jamie's window at half past seven that morning.

"That's not news," Jack reassured him. "They were only like that because they love you so much. Deep down, they'll be proud. Proud that someone who has come from the same streets as them has signed for Barcelona. Well, almost, anyway."

Neither Jack nor Jamie mentioned the medical but it was hanging there silently between them. The one final hurdle that Jamie had to overcome in order to become a Barcelona player.

"Look," said Jack, suddenly pointing out of the window. "Some of the mountains have still got snow on them."

Jamie knew what Jack was doing but he played along just the same.

"Oh, yeah," he said, poking his nose up against the

transparent plastic porthole. "So what mountain is that? Is it Everest?"

"Not unless we're going via India," laughed Jack. "You really didn't take much notice in geography, did you?"

"We're not all brainboxes like you, are we, Jacqueline?" Jamie retorted, his mind drifting back to when they were at school: Jack the most popular girl, in the top sets for everything, Jamie much more ordinary, except for his one special talent. The football computer in his head.

"Yeah, well, shame my brains aren't worth as much as your feet," teased Jack. "So, do you know what you're going to do with the money, then?"

"Yup!" Jamie announced proudly.

"What?" said Jack.

"Going to buy Mum and Jeremy a house," explained Jamie. "I told them this morning. They were well chuffed."

"Wow! I bet they were! What did they say?"

"Jeremy told me not be so stupid and said that I should save it. Typical him. Started banging on again about how unpredictable a footballer's career is and that I had to be careful, but I just said: 'Look, when it was just me and Mum, sometimes we had nothing, but she always made sure I had everything I needed, so this is just me saying thank you' … and then Mum started crying so Jeremy had no chance!"

At that moment, Jack leaned over and gave Jamie a very light kiss on the cheek and softly touched his knee. Jamie had no idea why she'd done it and it was finished almost as soon as it had begun.

Jamie looked out of the window again, staring along the line of the horizon. A white carpet of cloud led the way towards the bright, golden sun. A new world would be awaiting him when he stepped off this plane.

He imagined himself becoming one of the greatest players in the world. Playing for Barcelona … skinning defenders with his electric pace and wizard-like skills. Could it happen? Could it *really* happen?

Jamie flexed his knee, twisting it to the side to see how it felt. A twinge of pain but nothing he couldn't handle. Then he tilted his seat back, looked at Jack typing away on her laptop, and closed his eyes. If he could pass this medical, if his body could get through this final crucial test, his dreams and his reality would suddenly become almost the very same thing.

# ⑦

# The Medical

Had it not been for the army of security guards that Barcelona sent to meet them at the airport, Jamie and Jack might never have got out of the arrivals lounge.

It had been chaos. Hundreds of camera crews, all with presenters pushing a microphone in either Jamie or Jack's face. It seemed more like an attack than a welcome.

"How are you feeling?" asked Jack as they slipped into the back of the waiting people carrier.

Jamie just shook his head. It was too much for him to take in; too much to contemplate. And, on top of everything, the hardest part was yet to come.

"Thanks for coming with me," was all he could muster as the car sped ever closer to Barcelona's Stadium.

"Don't think I could do this without you."

"First, we will do the beep tests, then I will monitor your heart and after we shall do the scan of your bones," the Barcelona doctor told Jamie, almost before he had introduced himself.

The man had a strange accent and, for some unaccountable reason, Jamie took an almost instant dislike to him.

Perhaps it was because Jamie knew that this one man held the key to his entire future in his hands.

An hour later, Jamie was feeling far more confident. He'd nailed the beep tests and he knew it – he could see the astonishment in the doctor's face as he registered phenomenal times for his jogs and sprints. The doctor may have been surprised but Jamie was not. He had always been one of the fittest footballers around. Archie Fairclough, the assistant manager at Hawkstone, had once jokingly asked Jamie whether he had two hearts – so impressive were his levels of physical endurance.

"OK, now we come to the important part," said the doctor in a slow and calculating voice, before pointing to what looked like a white plastic coffin in the corner of the room. "If you lie down on the machine over there, we will now slide you into the scan. This will allow us to see your bones and joints – to check that everything is normal."

The three minutes that Jamie spent trapped inside that sealed capsule, listening to the laser lights beaming their way through his skin and inside his body, seemed to stretch to infinity. The thought that the machine had broken and that he would never be able to escape even crossed Jamie's mind. And all the while, he knew that the innermost weaknesses of his body were being laid bare to the doctor. Secrets were now impossible.

When the machine finally spat him back out, the doctor's face held exactly the same blank expression as before. He was giving nothing away.

"How does it all look?" Jamie asked, sitting back down and trying to hide his nerves.

"This knee," said the doctor, grabbing Jamie's left leg just above the shin. "Does it feel OK if I do this?"

And with that, he tried to twist Jamie's knee to the side. Instinctively, Jamie shouted in agony: "Aaagh!"

The doctor let go and Jamie clutched his knee back towards him, wincing in both pain and embarrassment.

He knew how to get through games, how to get through life, by protecting that knee, treating it like a precious jewel. Why had the doctor twisted it like some cheap toy?

It was at that moment that the doctor stood up and

left the room, without so much as telling Jamie where he was going.

Jamie put his trousers back on and slumped deep into the chair.

He knew something was wrong. Badly wrong.

# 8
## Results

Jamie told Godal everything.

Perhaps they already knew anyway; these clubs did months of research on players before they signed them. But that wasn't the reason Jamie started talking as soon as Godal came into the room the doctor had vacated.

It was more simple than that. He just knew he couldn't hide the truth any longer. If Jamie kept secrets inside, they just got bigger and bigger, grew into monsters and destroyed him from within.

Jamie didn't want that. If he was going to play for this club, he had to tell them everything about him. And just pray that they still wanted him after.

So he told Godal about the car accident three years before, which had crushed his knee. He told him about the reconstructive surgery which had rebuilt it and how the joint was now held in place by metal screws. And he told him about the series of injections that he had had in his knee to get him through the World Cup.

He told him that, these days, he could never play football without feeling pain.

But he also told Godal that it was OK. That he could handle it. That he could still be that special player that Barcelona were looking for.

Jamie searched Godal's face, trying to read his reactions. Godal had listened to Jamie and was looking at the doctor's notes. He was shaking his head.

"I like you, Jamie," he said finally. "I decided the first time I saw you play. You ran from your penalty area all the way to the goal and you ran so fast your feet did not even seem to touch the ground. I turned to my scout and I said: 'I have to have this player. He must come to Barça!'

"But this problem with your knee. This is worse than we thought. We knew about the knee operation, but we believed it was fixed. We did not know the problems it is still causing you. How can I turn to the president and fans – who own this club – and say that we are paying such a big transfer fee and such big wages to a player who cannot play football without pain?

"It wouldn't make sense, Jamie. I cannot be reckless

with the club's money. I would not buy a car that has a problem with the engine. So how can I buy a player who has a problem with his knee?

"The doctor here is very clear in his notes. He says your knee needs rest. That is your only chance to play football again without pain. He is a very good doctor, Jamie; you should listen to him. He says otherwise you could break down at any moment … that your knee is like 'a ticking bomb'…"

Jamie laughed. Not in joy but in desperation.

"I've heard all this stuff before," he said. Where did they all get this figure of six months' complete rest? There was no time for that.

"I've heard it from other doctors," repeated Jamie. "But I know my body better than anyone else, Señor Godal. I know what it's capable of and how to treat it."

But Godal only smiled weakly in return.

"The risk is too big, Jamie. We cannot pay so much for a player with such physical problems, no matter how good he is. I am sorry. I will call Hawkstone to tell them that the deal is off."

"No!" shouted Jamie. "Please! Just wait a second."

He knew, both for his sake and for Hawkstone's, that he could not let this deal slip through his fingers. He knew that there is never "another chance" with a club like Barcelona. You have one shot. Only one shot of playing for a club like that.

Jamie frantically searched for an answer and then, from somewhere, came up with an idea that was so ridiculous, so risky, that it might just have a chance of working.

"Señor Godal," began Jamie, sensing a feeling of euphoria lift up from his stomach, through to the rest of his body. He knew what a massive gamble he was about to take. "If you're worried about paying me lots of money and then me getting injured, why don't we do a deal that means that doesn't happen?"

Godal looked at Jamie quizzically before sitting back down.

"Go on," he said, leaning forward. "Tell me what you have in mind."

# 9
# A Kiss

Thirty-four steps down, deep into the heart of the cavernous belly of the stadium, then eight steps up, up and into the light...

Jamie Johnson walked out on to the pitch at the Nou Camp and looked up ... up ... and further up... The gigantic stands curved towards the sky on all sides, reaching so high it was almost impossible to see the top. No wonder the Barcelona players felt blessed to play for the club, Jamie thought to himself. They were pretty much being watched from the heavens.

This was his first chance to take in the full, wondrous grandeur of the stadium. He'd seen it on TV many times, but to be here, standing on the pitch, was completely different.

And now, after he and Godal had reached their unique agreement – albeit a highly risky one on both sides – Jamie could finally call himself a Barcelona player. This ground, this phenomenal piece of architecture, was his new footballing home.

"Jamie!" said one of the Barcelona press team, putting a club scarf around his neck. "The fans! They have come to see you! Why don't you show them something special?"

And with that, from somewhere a specially branded Barça football was launched at Jamie.

The twenty thousand fans in the stadium erupted with noise. This was what they had come to see: their precious new signing kicking a ball.

Immediately, Jamie's heart sang and his body smiled.

This was what he was here to do. There had been too much talk. Too much delay. Too many worries about knees and money. That wasn't what was important. This was.

Jamie accepted the ball on to the side of his shin before flashing his foot around it to trap the ball between his calf and the back of his thigh.

Instantly the fans responded, leaping to their feet to chant Jamie's name.

He smiled and back-heeled the ball all the way back over his head. He watched it loop on to his right foot and then gave it an almighty thump, rocketing a volley high into the air above him.

The camera flashes all captured the image of Jamie staring up into the sky, eye fixed firmly on the ball. Then, as the ball dropped, he arched his back, allowing his chest to cushion the ball high enough for it land on his forehead.

For an instant, he was back in his granddad Mike's garden, Mike clapping, urging him on, telling him to have fun with the football – to "show it you love it".

With the ball balancing on his head, Jamie turned to the cameras and, quickly tilting his chin up, let the ball drop on to his lips.

He kissed the Barça ball and, in that moment, with his joy at signing for his dream club clear for everyone to see, he began to win the hearts of his new fans.

Barcelona was already coming under Jamie Johnson's spell.

# 10
# Home

"You realize how big this gamble is, right?" asked Jack, as Jamie inputted the security code to open the door to his new apartment. "I mean, let's say you *do* get injured..."

"I had to find a way," replied Jamie. "I couldn't let this chance go. And anyway, what was the alternative? Go back to Hawkstone – after all the hype of me coming over here? I'd look like an idiot and Hawkstone would go bust. No way I'm letting that happen. Anyway, life doesn't look too bad from here, does it?"

And with that, Jamie opened the door to a new level of luxury.

Jamie was taking over the apartment that had been made vacant when Ivan Viduka, Barça's Croatian striker, had departed from the club to sign for Bayern Munich earlier this summer.

Overlooking the shimmering Barcelona coastline, it was the kind of home that you would normally see in the glossy magazines... And now it was Jamie's. And Jack's.

Jamie sprinted from room to room like an excited child. He flung open all the cupboards and switched on all the TVs at top volume.

Then he jumped on one of the huge double beds and stretched himself out as far as his body would go. There were only a couple of hours to settle in before he and Jack were expected back at the Nou Camp, as personal guests of the club president, to watch Barça's first home game of the season against Valencia in the Spanish Super Cup.

But before any of that, there was something else that Jamie needed to do. If he could just pluck up the courage.

He strode out on to the balcony and put his arm around Jack's shoulder. He looked into her dark brown eyes and tried to form the perfect sentence in his head.

Jamie opened his mouth but at first no words came out; nerves had stolen his speech. He took two deep breaths to steady himself and, as the scent of Jack's hair filled his senses, he prepared to make his second huge gamble of the day.

"Jack," he said. "I want us to... It's never quite... Can we make it ... proper between us out here? Will you be my girlfrien—"

Jamie's voice trailed off and he took a step back.

Immediately, he knew that something wasn't right. That Jack wasn't happy.

Jamie had made a big mistake. He had assumed that Jack would be staying with him in Spain.

"If that's what you were thinking, why didn't you ask me?" demanded Jack. She was angry. She didn't like people making decisions for her.

"I don't know. Everything was happening so quickly... I'm asking you now..."

"Jamie, my job is to report on English football. How can I do that from Spain?" she asked, checkmating Jamie with one simple move.

"Can't you report on Spanish football?"

"I don't speak Spanish, Jamie! It's all right for you. You score a goal and it means the same in any language. But I have to write about the goals and I need to do that in English."

"But I'm earning enough that you don't have to work," said Jamie. "Just stay and ... you can go shopping while I'm playing and then we can do stuff together after."

Jack placed her hands on her hips and glared at Jamie. No words were required. She was not interested in shopping. She was an achiever. She had her own career. And she was brilliant at her job. Which were, of course, many of the reasons that Jamie liked and respected her so much in the first place.

"But if I'm here and you're there," he stuttered, "what about …?"

"Friends," said Jack. "For now."

So, it turned out that Jack and Jamie only had one evening together in Barcelona and, despite Jamie's disappointment at what Jack had said, they still had a great night together. They spent it doing what they most enjoyed. It was what had brought them together in the first place and what would always keep them together.

Football.

## SPANISH SUPER CUP FINAL SECOND LEG

FC Barcelona 4 - 1 Valencia
Rodinaldo. 2, 32          Dorwardo. 18
Obi Ehiogu. 21
Bolo. 72

**Barcelona win the Spanish Super Cup 6-3 on aggregate**

"That was unreal! I've never seen skills like that!" Jamie purred as he and Jack got into the limousine to drop Jack at the airport so she could catch her late-night flight back to England. They had watched Barça put in a spellbinding performance to win their first trophy of the season and it was still only August.

It was only as they pulled up to the airport terminal that Jamie started to get upset. True, Jack would always be there on the end of the phone, but that would be nowhere near the same as what he had hoped for when he had plucked up the guts to talk to her on the balcony.

"They were good," smiled Jack, her elusive eyes refusing to reveal her own emotions. "But don't hero-worship them too much! You're training with them tomorrow. So now it's time for them to see how good *you* are…"

## 11

# Welcome

### Saturday 25 August – the day before
### Athletic Bilbao v Barcelona

There is no such phrase as *the early bird catches the worm* in Spanish and Jamie received his first lesson in his new culture at training the next morning.

Barcelona were gearing up for their first league match of the season – away at Athletic Bilbao – on Sunday night and Godal had told him that training began at ten a.m. Eager to impress, Jamie made sure he arrived at the training complex for nine a.m. and immediately began his warm-up routine.

In fact, it was almost eleven-thirty by the time Jamie's new teammates rolled into town.

They were hugging and talking about the game the night before, so happy to see one another that they barely registered the presence of their small, pale new teammate in the corner. Jamie felt invisible. In fact, he felt completely ordinary. All of his new teammates looked as much like models as they did footballers.

The ponytails, the immaculately groomed goatee beards, the tight white T-shirts, the necklaces and the overwhelming aroma of fresh aftershave. This was half dressing room, half catwalk.

Finally, it was the Brazilian magician, Rodinaldo, who strolled over to welcome Jamie. While Jamie aspired to become universally recognized as one of the best players in the world, Rodinaldo had already reached that level and, as he approached, Jamie could not help but notice the amazing physical condition the player was in.

The man was built like a prize fighter; muscles rippling everywhere. There was not an ounce of fat anywhere on his body.

Jamie had himself come a long way since the days of being a skinny ginger kid at school. He had done hours and hours of weights to build himself up and even tried yoga to loosen and stretch his muscles, but he would never look like Rodinaldo. The man was the perfect physical specimen.

"*Buenos dias!*" said Rodinaldo, his gleaming white teeth sparkling as he reached out his fist for Jamie to touch. "I ask Barça to bring you here to play with me! And you here! We make party together on football pitch!"

Now, as if following Rodinaldo's lead, the other Barça players came to introduce themselves too. High fives, pats on the back and hugs were coming from all directions.

There was Steffen Effenhegel, the tall, aristocratic-looking German centre-half who captained the team, offering Jamie the firmest of handshakes and a piercing look in the eye. And last to greet Jamie, the most mysterious and intriguing of all the Barcelona players: Major – short and squat in stature, with black hair and big childlike eyes. The story of Major was now almost mythical.

He had been an orphan brought up on the streets of Barcelona, kicking only rolled-up socks around the backstreets and alleyways of the city until, one day, the president of the club – on a goodwill visit to one of the centres for the homeless – had himself caught sight of this dirty boy with beautiful skills.

He had invited the young Major to join the rest of the Barcelona recruits at the famous La Massia Academy, where, along with perfecting his football, he had learnt to read and write.

Major, Jamie guessed, was the personification of what Godal had meant when he talked about Barça being *more than just a club*. Major had waited until the other players had gone out to training and now, wordlessly, he was taking Jamie's clenched fist and tapping it softly against his chest.

"Welcome to the family," he said in accented but clear English. "Now you are one of us."

# 12

# Training

Jamie sprinted as fast as his legs would take him. He turned on his own internal extra-burners, he switched on his turbo gear and yet, no matter how fast he pelted across the grass, the ball was always gone, just a millisecond before he could get there.

There Jamie stood, panting in the centre of a man-made circle. This was a piggy-in-the-middle warm-up game in which a player, standing in the middle of the circle, had to try to intercept the ball as it passed between the rest of the group. Once the player in the centre captured the ball, he was replaced by the one whose pass had given away possession.

It was not the first time that Jamie had played the game. Many coaches across the world used it, as it was not only a good way to warm up and get some light-hearted banter going, but at its core it promoted a vision of the game based around possession and quick, accurate, staccato passing.

In England, Jamie's pace alone would have meant that he could have got hold of the ball within one or two passes. Like a leopard in full flight, Jamie was almost always able to capture his prey.

However, now as he stood, gulping for air in the boiling midday sun, Jamie realized that he had already been the piggy in the middle for around ten minutes and, with each passing second, the howls of enjoyment from his new teammates seemed to get louder. They would wait until Jamie was right upon them, just about to seize control of the ball, before finding some wizard-like feint of the body or intricate piece of close control to move the ball on at the very last second.

Like a dog unable to stop chasing a ball, Jamie refused to give up, but he knew his strength was disappearing. He hoped his teammates might give him a break. But they would not – they simply carried on. Were they teaching him some kind of lesson? Were they trying to make him look stupid?

Jamie could feel his temples begin to pump with anger. Why had they all been so nice to him in the changing room only to mock him now on the pitch?

His fury began to inject extra pace and power into his running. No one could make him look foolish on a football pitch. This was his domain…

Hammering the ground, Jamie kept low and agile as he stalked the ball and then, when there was one momentary second of indecision, he pounced, sliding ferociously along the grass at top speed to push the ball out of the circle and slam into Steffen Effenhegel at the same time.

Effenhegel, having been knocked over, immediately jumped to his feet, staring over Jamie, who could sense a firm German punch about to come his way.

And then Effenhegel laughed and offered his hand to Jamie to lift him off the ground.

"Well done," said another voice from behind Jamie. It was Godal. He was dressed in a tracksuit with a whistle around his neck. "You lasted twelve minutes and forty-eight seconds. *And* you got the ball! That is a new record for a fresh signing. We do this with every player that comes to the club. It is a way of explaining our philosophy without words. We believe that, no matter how fast any player can run, the ball can always move faster. This is the way we play at Barça. This is why we love to pass the ball."

# Athletico Bilbao v Barcelona

## Sunday 26 August

Jamie was not in the team. He was a sub. Godal had told him the night before the game – just after Jamie had been made to stand on a table and sing a song in front of his new teammates.

It was one of many "initiation" routines that they had insisted on to mark his arrival at Barça. Strangest of all were the constant requests for Jamie to tell the other players the rudest word he knew in English. For millionaire footballers, Jamie thought they seemed a little overexcited about learning a new, rude word in a foreign language. And he wasn't quite sure whether they were just trying to get him in trouble so, in the end, he had a brainwave and told them that *nincompoop* was far and away the most disgusting piece of vocabulary to exist in the English language and made all his new teammates promise sincerely never to reveal to anyone that it was he who had taught them this horrendous word.

Although he was devastated not to be in the starting line-up for the game against Bilbao, Jamie had not really been able to argue. Barcelona had been superb against Valencia, so he could hardly demand the manager change a winning team.

As he went out on to the pitch to warm up with the rest of the players, Jamie immediately felt a rotten orange smash into the side of his face. At first he thought it was another prank by a teammate but then he looked around and saw that every one of the Barça players was being pelted with stinking fruit and vegetables. The food was mouldy and oozing a putrid, foul-smelling juice.

Not one of the players reacted, though. This must have been just the normal run of things. It was so different to England. There, the fans hurled abuse from the stands. Here, it was food. From all sides, the fruits were raining down, smashing into players' heads and faces, squishing the sickly-sweet juice on to their skin.

Jamie ran his sticky fingers through his hair. He could see the determination beginning to rise within his teammates. They were not smiling now. They were here to do the business.

Jamie watched from the bench as his new team continued their perfect start to the season, recording a comfortable 2-1 victory. Rodinaldo opened the scoring with a delicious drive before Major completed the job with an impish little chip.

However, while the celebrations flowed after the game, Jamie could not help but feel on the fringes of everything that was happening.

He clapped along with everyone else and tried to mouth the Spanish words that they were singing, but he could feel the distance between himself and the other players growing.

A dark flower of loneliness was beginning to open within him.

He was nothing more than an onlooker. He had to become part of this party.

# SPANISH LEAGUE

Athletic Bilbao 1 - 2 FC Barcelona
De Beristain, 82      Rodinaldo, 48
                  Major, 59

*Jamie Johnson unused substitute*

## Full set of weekly results:

| | | |
|---|---|---|
| Sporting Gijón | 1-3 | Atlético Madrid |
| Málaga | 4-2 | Valencia |
| Sevilla | 2-0 | Osasuna |
| Granada | 0-0 | Real Sociedad |
| Mallorca | 2-2 | Villarreal |
| Athletic Bilbao | 1-2 | Barcelona |
| Zaragoza | 3-4 | Betis |
| Getafe | 1-1 | Espanyol |
| Levante | 1-6 | Rayo Vallecano |
| Real Madrid | 4-0 | Racing Santander |

# 14

# Building Plans

## *Friday 31 August*

**From: Mum**
**To: JJ**
**Date: Friday 31 August, 12.34 p.m.**
**Subject:**

Hi JJ!

Thinking about you! What do you do out there when you're not playing football? Can't wait to hear your news.

I wanted to send you a picture of the new house. We're moving in next week! It's amazing. Neither Jeremy nor I can quite believe it.

We even played hide and seek in it today – it's that big! (Jeremy actually went and hid in the loft and stayed up there for two hours before I found him!)

Thank you so much, Jamie. From both of us. From the very bottom of our hearts. You know how proud we are of you.

Xmumx

P.S. – Can't wait to see you for the big game against Real Madrid! Jeremy searched for ages on the internet and got us a great deal on the flights!

P.P.S. – Your old school friend Dillon Simmonds popped round last night. It seems his brother, Robbie, was the person who threw the eggs at your window and Dillon brought little Robbie to apologize to us (was quite cute). Dillon said to say hi and it turns out he's doing some building/decorating these days (Jack's giving him a hand to set up the business) so he's going to help us do up the new place. Perfect timing, hey? I know I shouldn't say it, but he's turned into a very handsome young man too!

P.P.P.S. – Jack has literally just rung while I was writing this email to say that you will be coming home for a match soon? Sounds exciting! Can you stay with us? x

Jamie stood up and volleyed a tennis ball at the wall. He felt sick. What was all this business about Dillon Simmonds? At school, Dillon had been a bully of the worst kind. It seemed to have been his personal mission to make Jamie's life as miserable as possible. And now, not only was he helping decorate the new house, but he was spending time with Jack too! Where had all this come from? And, as for that stupid comment she'd made about Dillon being "handsome" now, well that was just too ugly for words.

It had made Jamie so angry that he almost didn't read the last couple of lines of the email but, when he sat back down at the computer and caught sight of those final words – "Coming back home for a game" – he almost leapt straight back out of his seat.

Going back to Hawkstone? That could only mean one thing! But it couldn't be true … could it?

Instantly, Jamie opened up a new browser window on his computer. His home page opened: the official website of Hawkstone United FC. And there it was. In huge letters.

The most perfect football match that Jamie Johnson could ever hope to play in.

## Hawkstone United 33,904

HAWKSTONE GET BARÇA

Hawkstone United have been drawn in the same group as Barcelona as we prepare for our first-ever taste of the Champions League.

Also in Group D are Galatasaray and Rosenborg (Champions of Turkey and Norway, respectively). However, it is the presence of Barcelona which has already captured the imagination of the fans, management and players alike.

"It's a tough group but we have to believe that we can progress," commented Hawks manager Harry Armstrong directly after the draw, which took place in Switzerland. "It's no secret that, as a club, we need to make some money this season, so progressing past the group stage becomes an even greater goal."

The two clubs have already been in close contact this summer, agreeing the largest transfer of the window to see Jamie Johnson trade the white and black of his hometown team for the blue and burgundy of the Catalan giants.

This was a fact not lost on skipper Glenn Richardson, who is looking forward to locking horns with Jamie when Barça come to town.

"The Champions League is the tournament every football player wants to be a part of," he admitted. "And I know Jamie is no different. When the games were on last season he used to come around to mine to watch it on my big screen. We always used to talk about what it would be like to play in it.

"I know our fans were disappointed to see him go but I'm sure, after everything he's done for this club, they'll give him a great reception when he comes back.

"But that's when the niceties will end. It'll be our job to stop him on the night – though we know better than anyone else how difficult that is going to be."

```
CHAMPIONS LEAGUE GROUP D
BARCELONA
GALATASARAY
HAWKSTONE UNITED
ROSENBORG
```

*Hawkstone United v Barcelona on September 26 is SOLD OUT. Tickets for all other home matches still available. Please contact the ticket office for details.*

# Bench Warmer

**_Wednesday 12 September – twelve days later_**

**_Barcelona v Galatasaray_**

**_First Champions League Group Game_**

Jamie had scored two stunning goals in two games.

For Scotland.

After ten days away, he had walked back into the Barcelona training complex feeling his whole body bulge with energy. Playing those two European Championship qualifiers against Serbia and Begium had got some running back into his legs and reminded him what it felt like to play again.

He was back on form and, what was more, in the next two weeks Barcelona were due to play against

BOTH Real Madrid and Hawkstone United.

Time had run out.

Jamie had to get into the team now.

The problem was, Juan Godal obviously didn't agree.

Even tonight, even when Barça had gone 3-0 up with twenty-six minutes still left to play, Godal had left him on the bench without so much as looking at him.

Barça had won their third successive match – this time starting their Champions League campaign in regal fashion – but Jamie's mood was blackening. If Godal always talked about the team being like a family, then why did Jamie feel like the illegitimate son that nobody wanted to acknowledge?

## CHAMPIONS LEAGUE

---

FC Barcelona 3 - 1 Galatasaray
Major. 16                    Artun. 70
Rodinaldo. 44
van der Kool. 64

---

### Jamie Johnson unused substitute

As he got dressed after the game, Jamie could feel the clock ticking in his mind. El Clásico was looming larger and larger on the horizon, and three days after that was an *even* bigger game for Jamie (if that was possible), the next Champions League group game against

Hawkstone. These were two matches he simply had to play in. If he stayed as sub, he might actually burst with frustration.

It was time to take action. Time for some straight talking.

"What do I need to do, Señor Godal?" Jamie asked, taking the seat next to Godal as the team went out for a late dinner together, as they tended to do after home games. "Please just tell me what I need to do to play and I'll do it. Whatever it is, you just have to say. Please."

Jamie stared at Godal. Sometimes his desire was so strong it produced a physical sensation – something like pain but closer to an ache – in his core.

His manager nodded. It was almost as though he had been waiting for Jamie to ask him this question.

"The first night we met. In London. Do you remember what I said about a player who comes to Barça, Jamie? What he must understand above everything else?"

"Yes," said Jamie instantly. He had replayed that meeting a million times in his head. "You said that Barça is *more* than a club. It is a spirit. And each new player must share that spirit."

"Good," said Godal. He wiped his mouth with his napkin and took a deep breath as he considered Jamie.

Then he gave an order that would completely transform Jamie's career at Barcelona.

"I want to see you smile."

# 16

# Stone Age

As with most of the best ideas in Jamie's life, it had actually been Jack's suggestion.

Naturally, Jamie had told her everything that Godal had said. Secretly, deep down, he had been hoping that she might say she would drop everything and come out to Spain to be with him. He really missed her in every way.

Although she had immediately promised to come out and see him in ten days' time, under the guise of writing a preview of the Barça–Hawkstone clash, they both knew she wouldn't be able to stay for longer than a day or so.

"But it does sound to me like Godal could be on to something," she had said. "If you're happy off the pitch, no one can stop you on it…"

Jack's voice dropped off. Jamie imagined her pacing up and down in her room, trying to unlock the code to this conundrum. And that was when she said it:

"When was the last time you spoke to Allie Stone?"

"Stonefish? Not for a few weeks," replied Jamie, kicking a tennis ball against the wall of his apartment. "I asked the Scotland boys what he was up to but none of them have heard from him since he retired."

"So hit him up. Give him a call," suggested Jack. "Could be just what you need. In fact, it could be exactly what you *both* need."

All of which was the reason that Jamie was now at his computer, composing an email. Even the subject line had started to make him laugh.

---

**From: Jamie Johnson**
**To: Allie Stone**
**Date: Wednesday 12 September, 9.26 p.m.**
**Subject: Get your big hairy, smelly bottom over here!**

Oi, Allie!
So I read in the papers that you've retired? You lazy layabout! How can you retire from being a goalkeeper? All you have to do is pick balls out of the net – are you too old to do that now? HA! HA!
OK, so I'm gonna give you the offer of a lifetime. I'm here in Barça in a four-bedroom flat overlooking the sea but my coach says I need someone to make me laugh, so obviously I thought of you, big boy! Just looking at you is enough to CRACK ME UP!!! Seriously, mate, it would be great to see you. I'm pretty bored out here and I reckon you could cheer me up. What do you say?
JJ

P.S. Can of baked beans in it for you.

P.P.S. No practical jokes. Don't start it. I'll batter you.

P.P.P.S. Stop picking the fluff out of your belly button – I CAN SEE YOU!

P.P.P.P.S. Has anyone actually ever written a P.P.P.P.S.?

Jamie smiled as he sent the email. He'd met Allie Stone during the World Cup and they had immediately struck up a bond. Not only had he been a great keeper but "Stonefish" was also one of the best friends Jamie had ever made through football. He had the warmest heart and the loudest fart that Jamie had ever witnessed.

So it was barely a surprise when only fifteen minutes later, Allie's name flashed up on Jamie's phone.

There was a text from the big man. And it was legendary.

# I'M UP FOR IT! The Stone Age is about to begin!!!

# (17)

# Party Time

**_Thursday 13 September_**

Jamie could feel Godal's eyes boring into him at training the next morning. They were searching through Jamie, looking for the spirit that would tell his manager he was truly ready to play.

Jamie had never experienced this kind of test before. Normally, his football was judged by goals and assists. Spirit was something much more difficult to measure.

Jamie was trying to work out what the actual definition of the word "spirit" meant as he left the training ground, which was why it took his brain a few seconds to actually recognize the huge friendly figure waiting for him astride a tiny moped.

Jamie had sent the email less than twenty-four hours ago and yet here, _already_, was big Allie Stone.

Not that Stonefish was alone – he was with none other than Rodinaldo and, amazingly, the two of them seemed to be sharing some hilarious joke, despite the fact that Rodinaldo could barely speak a word of English and Stonefish was hardly fluent in Portuguese.

As Jamie approached, the two new best friends exchanged a final belly laugh, a special handshake and what could only be interpreted as an agreement to meet up later.

"You took your time," said Stonefish, immediately turning the tables on Jamie – it was as though Jamie was the one coming to visit *him*.

"I had to get some physio," replied Jamie. "How did you get here so quick? And where's your luggage? And how do you know Rodinaldo?"

"Eh, what's with all the questions? You're not my mum!" laughed Allie, elbowing Rodinaldo in the ribs to get him to start laughing too. "I got on the first flight. Got in at eleven last night and met Roddy at the nightclub at two o'clock this morning. We had a blast. You should have come! Hop on – we need to head back to yours and get ready – Roddy's party starts in an hour!"

It was fair to say that Rodinaldo's parties were legendary. Not only did Godal know that they went on, he actively encouraged them. Apparently he had even turned up to a couple last season.

So, within two hours of Stonefish's arrival, he and Jamie, wearing their sunglasses, Hawaiian shirts and tropical shorts, entered the world of a Rodinaldo Fiesta.

The music was blaring. People were playing volleyball in the pool. Waiters carrying huge watermelons and drinks were mingling among the partying guests, who were all dancing as if their lives depended on it.

"Here," said Stonefish. "Hold this."

He handed Jamie his motorcycle helmet, which Jamie, like an idiot, accepted, and with that, Stonefish was off. First he tried his hand at the Macarena with about twenty girls by the massive, vibrating speakers, before swiftly and effortlessly becoming part of the human conga that was snaking its way around the pool.

Jamie collected an orange-looking drink from one of the waiters and took a moment to appreciate the surroundings.

Big palm trees with drooping, friendly leaves offered shade from the warm sun. A picture-perfect swimming pool shimmered as the waves from the volleyball game caused the water to slap against the marble tiles.

Jamie thought back to the days – the beautiful British summer days – when everyone was happy, when everyone had a smile on their face and the world seemed a quite wondrous place. Five or maybe six times a year, you might get a day like that in England. It seemed to Jamie that every day in Barcelona was like that. Or at least could be.

It was at that moment that Rodinaldo decided to join his own party. Dressed impeccably in a stunning cream suit, he appeared on the terrace above the revellers and raised his hands before getting behind the decks to start DJing.

Then, as he spun the tracks, he gave a demonstration of the full array of his football talents.

Rodinaldo had perfected the ability to disco dance while keeping a ball aloft in the air. It was a truly bewitching sight, worthy of a TV show all of its own.

With the music blasting, the Brazilian's feet moved in flashes, keeping the ball up in time to the rhythm. And that was when it clicked for Jamie. He'd been trying to work it out ever since he'd seen Rodinaldo play. *What was different about him? Where did he get that extra-special movement from? How did he manage to play the game on a different canvas to everyone else?*

Now Jamie could see it. Rodinaldo played football in the same way that he danced: to the beat.

"Oi!" said Stonefish, grabbing Jamie by the collar and hauling him into the centre of the conga as they went past. "Come join the party!"

Jamie needed his hands free to grab the person in front of him, so there was only one thing for it: he put the helmet on his head, pulled the visor down and joined in.

## Friday 14 September

The rhythm was still pumping through Jamie in training the next day. And it felt good.

One touch – one small, spinning nick off the outside of Jamie's boot to set up Major for a sweet strike even drew applause from Godal. That almost never happened. At most, Jamie had heard Godal emit a kind of birdlike whistle when he admired a move or a passing sequence but, following this flick, Godal had actually briefly stopped the game to explain to the other players why Jamie's touch had been so effective.

"You see," he'd stated, wrapping his arm around Jamie as he spoke. "With one stroke of the ball, he has killed three defenders. Bravo!"

That was the moment that Jamie sensed it.

He was going to be in the team on Sunday. And what was more, he had a feeling in his boots that he was going to do something special.

# Playing to the Beat

**Sunday 16 September**

**Spanish League**

Mallorca v FC Barcelona
14 MINUTES PLAYED

Jamie collected the ball and turned in the same movement. This was his first real chance to run with the ball and he wasn't going to waste it.

He sprang forward as if it were the start of a hundred-metre sprint, keeping the ball nice and close as he surged across the turf. As the defender came to confront him, in the corner of his eye he spotted Major free slipping him the ball and racing to the other side of the defender.

Accelerating back on to Major's return pass, Jamie unleashed an instant strike, which roared in from the millisecond it left Jamie's boot. The ball exploded into the roof of the net with such ferocious venom that the goalkeeper made only the pretence of attempting to save it about a second after it had flashed past him.

---

### Mallorca 0 - 1 FC Barcelona
Johnson. 16

---

Jamie wheeled away in delight. He knew what he'd done. He knew that this strike would be played on TVs in countries all over the world. Now people would know that he had truly arrived at Barcelona.

And at the same time, this was not Jamie's goal alone. Immediately, he went to hug Major and Rodinaldo, and the three of them – arm in arm – then jogged joyously over to share the celebrations with Godal.

Jamie looked up at the travelling Barcelona fans – the new members of his family – and felt his heart heave with pride.

This truly was a beautiful game and it was exactly, unmistakably what he had been put on this earth to do.

And nothing could ever change that.

Or at least that was what he thought.

## *Final Score Spanish League*

Mallorca 1 - 4 FC Barcelona
Raymondo, 77    Johnson, 16, 32, 80
                Rodinaldo, 42 (pen)

## *Jamie Johnson scores a hat-trick on his debut for Barcelona*

## *Top of the Spanish League Table:*

| Club | Played | Points | Won | Drawn | Lost | For | Against |
|------|--------|--------|-----|-------|------|-----|---------|
| Real Madrid | 3 | 9 | 3 | 0 | 0 | 11 | 2 |
| Barcelona | 2 | 6 | 2 | 0 | 0 | 6 | 2 |
| A Bilbao | 3 | 6 | 2 | 0 | 1 | 6 | 3 |

# ㉒⓪
# Headline-Maker

**Thursday 20 September – four days later**

Jamie felt as happy as he had ever been.

He was smiling inside as he fired up his computer and typed the words "Jack Marshall", "interview", and "Jamie Johnson" into the search engine.

It was two-thirty a.m. He knew that was the time that the articles for the next day's newspapers appeared on the websites.

He couldn't wait to see what Jack had written.

* * *

# NO MORE PAIN IN SPAIN

## Jamie Johnson WORLD EXCLUSIVE by Jacqueline Marshall

"Hi! My name's Jamie Johnson. Do you like football?"

That was how the small, skinny ginger boy introduced himself on the day that my family and I moved in across the road to where he lived twelve years ago.

"Hello," I responded. "My name's Jack Marshall. No, I don't like football, I love it, and I bet you a milkshake you can't score a penalty against me."

I lost the bet. Well, how was I supposed to know that I was talking to a kid who would grow up to be one of the best and most exciting players in the world? You can't blame a girl for having a little bit of confidence.

Fast forward twelve years and the skinny boy from Hawkstone has turned into a fully fledged football megastar with Barcelona. After a frustrating period out of the team, Johnson announced his talent to the Spanish public with a stunning hat-trick – including a trademark overhead kick – on his Barcelona debut last weekend and now looks set to play in both the Clasico and the Champions League during a pivotal week ahead for his club. So was he always confident that swapping Hawkstone for Catalonia was the right move?

"It wasn't easy at the beginning," admits Johnson. "I missed everyone back home and I couldn't speak the language either. I went to the shop one day to buy some eggs and then I realized that I didn't know the Spanish word for them. In the end, I had to stand there, clucking away, pretending to be a chicken, miming like something was coming out of my bum. They thought I was a bit weird at first until someone else in the shop who spoke English told them what I wanted!

"Not being in the team was tough too. But I guess I've got used to things not being easy for me. I've always had to battle. At school people used to have a go about my ginger hair, and then on the football pitch defenders would try to kick lumps out of me to try to scare me, but I learned pretty early that the best way to stop them doing that is to get up straight away and pretend that I didn't even feel a thing. My granddad taught me that. He used to tell me that 'even if they've torn you in half, you still bounce straight back up like it's nothing'. That was one of the best bits of advice I ever had."

"How important is family?" I ask Jamie. He shifts uncomfortably at first. It is an open secret that he does not talk to his father and chooses to go by the family name of his mother (Johnson) as opposed to the Reacher surname which is actually on his birth certificate.

"Family and friends are massive for me," Jamie says, after a period of silence. "It might sound strange to say it but in real life, outside of football, I'm not that confident. I'm not that clever and I'm not that good with words and stuff. I just like being around people I know and trust. And who make me laugh."

Back on the pitch, it looks set to be the biggest couple of weeks in his career to date. With an estimated TV audience of five hundred million people expected to tune in to next week's El Clasico with Real Madrid, followed by a Champions League tie against none other than his beloved Hawkstone United, Johnson really is living out every football fan's fantasy.

So, is he prepared to reveal the secret of his success to the millions of young Jamie Johnsons out there, all desperate to follow in his footsteps?

"The secret is ... there's no secret," he states. "The harder you work, the luckier you get."

* * *

Jacqueline Marshall was speaking to Jamie Johnson at the Barcelona training ground. Jamie Johnson asked that his fee for this interview be donated to charity.

Competition – win tickets to see Hawkstone United v Barcelona in the Champions League! To stand a chance of winning a pair of tickets to watch Jamie Johnson playing against his old club, simply tell us: what is Jamie Johnson's middle name?
a) Colin
b) Cyril
c) Michael

Details of how to enter below.
Winners will be announced in tomorrow's paper.

\* \* \*

Jack was a brilliant writer. It was a seriously good piece.

But that was not why Jamie was smiling. His spirit was glowing because of something completely different. Something that had happened after the interview.

The interview had taken place yesterday in one of the cafes on the beach, and when Jack had put her notepad away, they'd gone for a walk by the sea. It was then that, without any warning at all, Jack had turned to Jamie and said: "Sorry for being such an idiot last time I was here. It doesn't matter how far away we are. Of course I'll be your girlfriend."

And then she had kissed him.
Properly.

# To the Letter

### Friday 21 September

Dear Jamie Johnson,

You will probably never read this because you are one of the best players in the world.

My friend Dexter said that first goal you scored against Mallorca was one was so powerful it would have broken two sets of goal nets! And the overhead kick — that was insane!

Anyway, I don't care whether you read this or never reply to me because I just wanted to write down how amazing you are at football. When I watch you play, it makes me so happy. Your skills are so wicked. You are my football hero. So, I wanted to know, who is your football hero?

Please write back even if it's only in ten years' time (after you have read all the other thousands of letters that you must get every day).

From your number one fan (I know everyone says that but I really mean it. I am your biggest fan).

Alex Riley (aged 13)

P.S. Do you think that they will ever make a film of your life? And if they do, who would you like to play you?

Jamie smiled. If he ever got down or depressed, reading a letter like this was all he needed to get him back on top form. And with Stonefish now able to help weed out the weird letters (one woman in Norwich had started sending him pictures of her cat) Jamie only got to see the nice ones. Like the letter from Alex.

Immediately, Jamie picked up a pen. It was his special yellow FIFA pen that they had sent to him all the way from Switzerland after he had played at the World Cup.

He made sure that he wrote in his neatest handwriting, as he had a feeling Alex would be showing this letter to all his mates, especially Dexter!

Dear Alex,

Thank you so much for your letter, which made me very happy.

It actually reminded me a bit of myself. I used to write letters all the time to the Hawkstone players and when I got a letter back from them it was a brilliant feeling, so I hope you like this letter from me...

To answer your question, my football hero is someone who you won't have heard of, but that doesn't stop him being a hero. It's a man called Mike Johnson, who was my granddad. He was a brilliant footballer and would have been a top professional if he hadn't got a really bad knee injury. He's the one who introduced me to football and got me to love it. I often think about him when I play.

As for who would play me in a film of my life, that's a great question! I think that

But before Jamie could write down his answer, he suddenly became aware that Stonefish was standing over him holding another letter in his hand.

"I think you need to look at this one, mate," he said solemnly. It was the most serious Stonefish had ever looked in his life. "It came a few days ago."

He slowly placed the letter down on the table in front of Jamie.

Jamie,

I don't know any other way to say this. I need your help.

I've ~~can't~~ got myself into some problems here in England. And it's not looking good. I owe ~~a x~~ some money to the wrong kind of people, and if I don't pay them back soon ... well, it ain't gonna end pretty. Can you send me some money? Just a couple of thousand. I'll pay you back, I promise. I wouldn't ask if it wasn't desperate.

I know there's no reason for you to help me. I guess I'm just hoping that you might want to help out your old man. Please, Jamie?

Your,

Dad

P.S. Here's my new number: 07~~212~~ 456 982

"He's lying," said Jamie, angrily crunching up the letter and chucking it in the bin. "He's not in trouble, he just can't be bothered to work. Seen it a thousand times before."

"How do you know that, bud?" asked Allie, attempting to rescue the letter from the bin. "Maybe he's telling the truth. He sent this letter ten days ago, you know? Sometimes it's good to sort this stuff out before it's … too late."

"He's the one who's too late," stormed Jamie. "He left me and my mum with nothing but a load of debt that he ran up on credit cards. Trust me, Stonefish. The only time he's ever been interested in me was when he wanted something. Leopards don't change their spots."

# The Build-Up

## Saturday 22 September – the day before
## Barcelona v Real Madrid

Jamie gave his mum a massive hug. He didn't do it
enough, he knew.

He was around the age of twelve when his mum had
asked one day why he'd stopped hugging her as much
he used to. He'd shrugged his shoulders and felt bad –
he knew how much she liked to get a hug from him.

It was great to see her and Jeremy. They brought
that feeling of home with them and they made Jamie
laugh too. Even though he had offered for them to stay
with him and Stonefish or to put them up in one of the
nicest hotels in the city, they had insisted on renting
a cheap little apartment by the railway station. They'd

95

also already planned out their whole itinerary for the four days that they were in Barcelona. As far as Jamie could tell, it looked like they were going for the world record for the number of museums visited in one holiday.

"Jack says hi, by the way." His mum smiled. Jamie wondered whether she knew that he and Jack were together properly now. But he didn't ask. He just handed over the match tickets to Jeremy.

"This is a big old soccer game, isn't it?" said Jamie's stepfather as he opened the envelope to look at the tickets.

"What? Barcelona v Madrid?" said Jamie ironically. "Only about the biggest match in the world!"

With the match now only twenty-four hours away, the build-up was beginning to reach astronomic levels. Only today, the two coaches had held a joint press conference in which the sparks had begun to fly.

"The Barcelona team are used to having everything their own way. But tomorrow night, they will not have it easy," Fernando Nemisar, the Madrid coach, had warned, indulging in his usual pre-match psychological warfare. He had even turned to look Godal directly in the face, saying: "We are not scared of your ability to pass, because we can pass better … and not only that. We are stronger, faster and hungrier than your players."

The press, lapping up every word of this drama, had

quickly asked Godal for a response. They wanted the two men to confront each other but the Barça manager refused to play ball.

"For him, attention is his oxygen," explained Godal, staring straight ahead, purposely ignoring Nemisar's presence. "For us – for my players – we live by another means. We live from keeping the football."

"So, just remind me," said Jamie's mum. "Because I keep on getting it mixed up. Which colour is Barcelona and which is Real Madrid?"

Jamie laughed and gave her a kiss on the cheek. He was about to play in a football match that would be watched in every continent around the globe. But he would never get too big for his boots while his mum was around.

# Crime and Punishment

## Sunday 23 September

# PRISON SHAME FOR JOHNSON FATHER

World Exclusive: Barry Digmore

The father of superstar footballer Jamie Johnson was last night facing a prison sentence, having been caught attempting to burgle Hawkstone midfielder Glenn Richardson's house while the player was involved in a Premier League match for his club.

Ian Reacher, 42, was discovered breaking into the football star's house on the outskirts of Hawkstone at 9.42 p.m. last night.

This is the latest in a long line of misdemeanours by the estranged father of the 19-year-old Barcelona star Jamie Johnson (real name Jamie Reacher).

The pair have not spoken for three years and the news will come as a major embarrassment for Johnson, who is preparing to face Real Madrid this evening before returning to Hawkstone next week for the eagerly awaited clash with his old side in the Champions League.

Jose Luis Armando Godal put the printed copy of the English newspaper story down in front of Jamie.

It was twelve-thirty p.m. Exactly eight and a half hours before El Clasico was due to kick off.

"I am so sorry, Jamie," he said, resting his hand lightly on Jamie's shoulder. "This is not a true father."

Jamie nodded in agreement. He was still furious at that person – he could no longer call him his "dad" – for putting him in this position. And why did he still feel embarrassed when he had nothing to do with this man?

"I can see how deeply this is affecting you," continued Godal. "So I am going to give you two weeks off to recover your calmness."

Jamie leapt up from his seat, his head banging with anger.

"No!" he yelled, looking for a door to punch, anything to let out the anger. "No," he repeated. "Señor Godal! You can't do this to me. You can't punish me – I haven't done anything wrong!"

"I am not punishing you, Jamie. I am protecting you."

The more worked up Jamie became, the calmer Godal seemed to act.

"You must trust me, Jamie," he continued in soft, measured terms. "I know football and, if you allow me to say it, I think I know you too. I know that for you, football and life are the same thing, so we cannot pretend that this has not happened. I look at you now and see you have a cauldron inside you. This is the time – when your head is not clear – that problems can happen on the pitch... And we must remember the deal that we made too, Jamie. You are not in the same position as the other players."

Godal stood up. For him the meeting was finished.

But for Jamie it was not.

"Señor Godal," he countered – immediately understanding that what he said at this very moment, the words he used right now, could have the most profound effect on his career. "I understand what you are saying, but I have only just got into this team. And now we have El Clasico and the match against Hawkstone. These aren't just *two games*. They are the biggest games of my life. I refuse to let you take me out of the team."

Godal shook his head.

"You are perhaps the most ambitious, passionate player that I have met," he said. It didn't sound quite like the compliment that it could have been. "I will play you, but I must tell you that ambition can be a curse as much as a blessing."

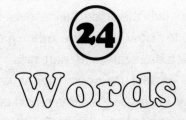

**24**

# Words

## *Ninety minutes until kick-off*

JACK MOB
Good luck for Clasico! I'm watching the
game on the TV and doing live text
commentary for the newspaper website!
Give it everything you've got (that way you
won't have enough energy to give Hawks
too much of a thrashing on Weds). It'll be
soooo weird seeing you play at Hawkstone
– for the opposition.
Jx
P.S. I'm REALLY looking forward to seeing
you after the game on Wednesday night.
P.P.S. No need to be nervous for Clasico...
It's just a game. J :)

Jack always repeated that phrase – "It's just a game" – when she could tell Jamie was nervous about a match. Of course they both knew it wasn't true, but somehow when Jack said it, it soothed Jamie's concerns.

Jamie could feel the smile taking over his face but he tried not to show it, as the other players would immediately latch on to it and start mocking him. The Barça players all said they could tell whenever Jamie was texting Jack because the same stupid grin appeared on his face every time! On a couple of occasions he'd even been forced to call them all a bunch of nincompoops because they had teased him so much.

Jamie touched his lips. Sure enough, they were curving upwards, lifted by Jack's words, and the fact that he only had three more sleeps before he would get to see her.

He allowed himself one final look at the text before he turned off his phone and put it into his locker.

It was time get changed.

It was time to get serious.

It was time to play Real Madrid.

# El Clasico

**Live text commentary of the game
by Jack Marshall...
Barcelona v Real Madrid
Kick-Off 21:00**

**20.45**
The Madrid and Barcelona players exit from their changing rooms and walk along the small, almost claustrophobic passageway, which is lined with paintings of former players.

A few teammates from the Spanish national team stretch their hands across the divide and produce small smiles to hide their glaring, grinding aggression.

Now the twenty-two players, separated by the iron grid, walk down the tunnel.

Thirty-four steps down, into the very depths of the foundations, and then eight steps up. Eight steps up towards the light. Towards the noise. Towards the pitch. Towards El Clasico.

## 20.59

The old stadium shudders as the referee prepares to start the game. Everyone is in the ground: celebrities, sports stars, the king of Spain ... and five hundred million people all watching around the world ... all waiting for the start.

## 21.00

The referee blows his whistle. El Clasico is under way! The noise sounds like thunder reverberating from the depths of the earth, and then ... football.

## KICK-OFF

Almost immediately the pattern for the game is set: Barcelona's quick, staccato passing pitched against Madrid's aggressive pressing.

Barça look the more comfortable side until, in only the third minute, disaster strikes...

Effenhegel passes the ball back to Dominguez, the Barcelona keeper... Adhering to Godal's principles of passing to retain possession, Dominguez attempts to chip the ball back to Effenhegel, but the Madrid forward line sense his plans and swarm around Effenhegel like hungry hyenas scenting a kill.

Quickly they dispossess the defender and bear down on the helpless keeper. One more predatory touch from Rosseri and the ball is in the net. First blood to Madrid.

---

FC Barcelona 0 - 1 Real Madrid
Rosseri, 4

---

The Nou Camp is silent.

Only on the touchline, where Nemisar runs the entire length of the pitch in a series of ostentatious fist-pumping celebrations, is the Madrid joy fully fledged.

Godal, sensing his players' need for direction, steps out of his technical area to let his team see their leader. He looks unruffled. Unfazed. Unmoved.

"Pass!" he shouts, moving his hands in different directions across his body to indicate the speed and tempo at which he wants the ball to be manoeuvred.

For a second Godal and Nemisar face each other. They look like two brothers. The same but different.

And then, immediately, battle recommences. 6 minutes played…

Once again the ball is passed back to Dominguez. The stadium takes a collective breath. He takes a touch of the ball and this time half-volleys it diagonally out to the right to Major. It's a stunning pass. A technique of which any outfield player in the world would have been proud.

Godal, in full view of Nemisar, claps his keeper's bravery in taking on the pass. 12 minutes…

And now here is Jamie Johnson. It's the first time he has got on the ball. He finds a yard of space and darts forward, keeping his body close to the ground and the ball magnetized to his boot. He is on the touchline, tight to the edge of the pitch. A defender comes to close him down. Johnson moves as if to lay the ball back to the full-back and then, right at the last minute, produces a turn to bewitch and mesmerize his opponent. The Barça fans roar their approval.

19 minutes...

The first bookings of the game come when Rodinaldo is callously hauled down on the edge of the penalty area. He stands up, puffs out his chest and pushes the Madrid man backwards. The Madrid defender exaggerates the extent of the contact and is told to stand up by the referee. Both players are given yellow cards. Rodinaldo's face is taut with anger and tension. There are no carefree smiles from the Brazilian today. He is focused on the prize.

23 minutes...

Now Major beats a man and slides the ball in for Johnson before going for the return. Johnson instead tries to beat his man and loses possession. The fans howl their disapproval. Godal rises and puts his fingers to his mouth. He whistles to get his new signing's attention. We can see him mouth those key words: "Pass and move." Johnson raises his hand in apology to his coach and his teammate. He understands.

27 minutes...

Suddenly, like a flash, Rodinaldo has dashed in to steal the ball from a Madrid midfielder like a robber in the night. He is accelerating away with the speed of an Olympic sprinter and then ... his ankles are tapped and he crashes to the ground.

The referee points to the penalty spot. Nemisar falls to the ground clutching his face before getting up to chide the Fourth Official. It is no use. The referee will not be changing his mind.

Rodinaldo picks up the ball and kisses it. He places it on the spot. He crosses himself as he takes three steps back.

He moves towards the ball, staring obviously at the right-hand corner of the net. He dummies to kick the ball, allowing the keeper to fall to the ground before calmly rolling the ball along the ground into the left-hand corner.

The stands shake in response. The cheers can be heard from miles away.

The game is, once again, all level.

---

FC Barcelona 1 - 1 Real Madrid
Rodinaldo, 29 (pen)     Rosseri, 4

---

The Brazilian's smile returns. He searches for Jamie Johnson and conducts an elaborate handshake routine, followed by a short samba dance. The pair have found their attacking harmony. They play to the same rhythm.

32 minutes...

The tackles snipe in like bullets. Barça players go down hurt. Madrid players haul them up and wag their fingers, telling them not to play-act.

The managers stand beside each other on the touchline, the simmering tension between them barely invisible.

36 minutes...

Now Barcelona break again. A quick one-two between Major and Rodinaldo. A yard of space is earned. Instantly, the ball is spread to the wing, where Johnson takes the pace of the move up another octave. He flies past one challenge before playing the ball back inside to Major. The little maestro produces a three-hundred-and-sixty-degree turn before flicking the ball into space on the left wing.

Now Johnson is free. Now he can use

that turn of pace. He is the furthest man forward. He strains every muscle, every tendon in his body to produce a run of such intense speed that the Madrid defence appears to dissolve in front of him.

The crowd rise in response to Johnson's balance, bravery and talent.

He reaches the edge of the area. The goalkeeper comes out to close him down.

For a second, the world stops.

Then Johnson knocks the ball past him, on the angle.

Now he chases after the ball, but it has gone too far wide. There is only one way for him to get the ball on target now...

In an almost impossible move, whilst still running, Johnson wraps his left foot around the front of his right and swings his heel backwards towards the ball.

It is an exquisite back-heel, which sends the ball hard and low along the ground towards the goal.

The goalkeeper turns and scrambles along the ground, trying to reach the ball.

The entire ground is frozen in time. No one dares move.

Except for Jamie Johnson.

Because he already knows.

---

## FC Barcelona 1 - 1 Real Madrid
Rodinaldo, 29 (pen)    Rosseri, 4
Johnson, 41

---

Seeing the ball hit the back of net, Jamie became a flaming ball of ecstasy. The joy sizzled through him like a lightning strike and suddenly Jamie found himself doing a celebration that he had never even tried before.

He did a double backflip!

The crowd gave a tumultuous roar of approval. However, almost as soon as he landed back on the ground, Jamie could feel his knee jar. He'd hurt it.

Badly.


42 minutes...

The Barça players are starting to enjoy themselves. They pass and then run to find space ... then they collect the ball again and move it on before the tackle can arrive.

It is a magic trick. They show Madrid the ball and then make it disappear without the opposition knowing where it has gone.

But not everything is looking so good. Jamie Johnson seems to be struggling. He is limping.

Godal immediately orders his substitutes to warm-up. He looks like he is going to make the change.

When Jamie saw the activity on the sideline and Max Muller getting changed to come on, he simply shook his head.

There was no way he was going to allow the ticking time bomb of his knee injury to explode today. No way he was going to come off now. No way.

He sprinted back to defend the corner, deadly determined to show Godal that he could carry on. That he could still give absolutely everything for this team.

44 minutes...

A corner to Madrid just before half-time. They send their formidable defenders up from the back, sensing this is their chance to hurt Barça. To wound them.

Barça pull every player back. Now is the time to stand together.

The ball is arced in. Dominguez jumps and punches the ball away but it doesn't go far. It lands on the penalty spot and bounces into the air.

The Madrid attacker lines it up. He watches it drop. He is going to volley it.

But Johnson reads the mind of the striker. He bravely dives to head the ball clear, knocking it to safety. It is a goal-saving intervention.

But the Madrid attacker cannot pull out of the shot. He follows through, crashing his boot into Johnson's skull with fearful power.

The referee immediately blows his whistle to halt the game.

Players from both teams stand over the stricken Johnson. The Madrid striker covers his eyes. He knows how hard he kicked his fellow player in the head.

The television cameras pan up to the stands. They show a worried-looking woman. She is Johnson's mother. She has come over to watch the game.

The paramedics, wearing their fluorescent yellow tops, rush on to the pitch with a stretcher...

But amazingly, and to everyone's relief, Johnson stands up, pushes them away and somehow even stays on the pitch to play the last few moments of the first half.

Jamie had been so desperate to stay on that he had refused to show how hurt he had been by the kick to his head.

It was only when he reached the Barcelona changing room and went to sit down that his body and brain collectively felt the full impact of his injury.

At first, he thought he was going to be sick.

As the nausea spread through him, he stood up in the middle of Godal's team-talk to go to the toilet. But as soon as he did his entire body felt wobbly and unstable. His legs buckled beneath him.

He was unconscious before his body collapsed on to the hard tiled floor.

# Part
# Two

## (26) Name

### *Wednesday 26 September – three days later*

The patient opens his eyes. He does not know where he is, what he is doing here or who these people are.

"Hello," says the doctor kindly. "Try not to worry. You've been unconscious for quite a long time and you have just woken up. Do you know what your name is?"

Panic spreads through the patient. He searches his mind but feels only pain.

"My name ... is ... I ... can't..."

The doctor purses his lips and rests his hand on his patient's shoulder and, as he does so, the patient passes out once more.

The patient is Jamie Johnson and he has been in a coma for three days.

*

"He's awake again!" shouted Jamie's mum, scrambling into the corridor of the hospital. "And he knows who I am!"

Jamie had just woken up for the second time and immediately recognized his mum.

"Where am I, Mum?" he'd asked, grabbing her hand.

Quickly the doctor reappeared, followed by two colleagues.

"I'm just going to ask you a few questions," said the doctor. "And don't worry if you don't know the answers. This is just to give us a little more information. Now, can you tell me what your name is?"

"Jamie Johnson," said Jamie.

He watched his mum close her eyes and breathe out of her mouth. Relief.

"Good," said the doctor. "Can you tell me the names of the two people in this room?"

Jamie smiled at his mum, who was holding his hand.

"Yup. This is my mum, Karen. And that's my stepdad, Jeremy."

"Excellent," continued the doctor, adding another tick to his list. "Just a few more, please, if you'll bear with me... How old are you?"

"I'm nineteen years old."

"Which school did you go to?"

"Kingfield."

"Where were you born?"

"Hawkstone."

"And what do you do for a living?"

"I'm a footballer."

Jamie looked around his hospital room. It was bedecked with hundreds of football scarves, cards and photos.

"And who do you play for?"

"I play for Hawkstone United," Jamie announced proudly.

# ㉗
# Old and New

**_Thursday 4 October – eight days later_**

"So this is it." Jamie's mum smiled proudly as she helped Jamie into his new bedroom.

They had returned to England as soon as the doctor had given them the all-clear that Jamie was OK to take the flight.

The week since Jamie had woken up had involved a series of tests to determine his injury and the damage done.

Finally, two days ago, the Spanish doctor had explained it all.

"You took a huge blow to the skull," he had confirmed, speaking perfect English. "This sent you into a coma for three days. Thankfully, there was no blood on the brain, so your life was not at risk, but you have been left with amnesia. It seems you have lost the memory of the last month of your life, or, to be more precise, everything that has happened since you moved to Spain."

Jamie had nodded. People had told him he was now a Barcelona player and their manager had even come to see him in hospital. And yet, no matter how hard he tried, he simply could not recall one second of his time in Spain.

Being told that he was a Barcelona player was like being told he owned a brand new Ferrari but that he was not allowed to drive it.

"When will I get my memory back and when can I start playing again?" Jamie had asked the doctor. He wanted to play for Barcelona as quickly as possible. He wanted to get back to the life that he couldn't remember.

The doctor had smiled enigmatically.

"This is not like another injury. It is not a broken bone that we can fix. It is not a torn ligament that we can repair. Where the brain is involved we have to be very careful indeed. There are no absolute rules and each case is different. You may or may not be lucky enough to recapture those memories. And your body may or may not be able to reach the same level of performance as it did before. Right now, we need to concentrate on getting you to walk properly again. And if it's what your family wants, I'm quite happy for you to do that back in England. I have told Barcelona this and they are happy too."

So here Jamie was in a brand new house that he did not recognize, with a pair of crutches by the door. And somewhere in his brain was the story of his time in Barcelona. The mass of memories that he was simply unable to recall.

Would they come back? Would he be able to remember those days at all? And when would he next be able to kick a ball?

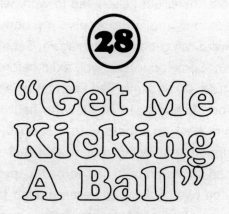

# 28

# "Get Me Kicking A Ball"

## Friday 5 October

"Hi Archie, it's Jamie Johnson."

Jamie was still in bed, but he'd called the Hawkstone Assistant Manager as soon as he'd woken up.

"Jamie!" said Archie. "How are you? I heard you were back. I was going to come and see you straight after training. How are you doing, son?"

"It'll take time, but I'll get there. Actually ... that's why I'm calling. I wanted to ask you if you could help me. Like you did when I was injured before."

Silence.

"Jamie. I'd do anything for you, you know I would. But I'm not a doctor or a physiotherapist."

"I know and don't worry – they've set me up with a doctor over here. But I also need to work with someone who knows me. Who knows my body. I need someone who can get me running again. Get me kicking a ball again. Come on, Archie, you did it before."

It was true. When Jamie had been hit by a car three years before, it had been Archie who had personally coaxed him back to fitness with a specially devised exercise and strengthening routine that had set Jamie on the road to stardom. It had forged a special bond between the two of them and even though this was a different type of injury altogether, Jamie was absolutely convinced that Archie could do it again.

"I really need you, Archie," he pleaded.

"You're a Barcelona player, not a Hawkstone one … we have to remember that. But I'll call Godal and see what he says," promised Archie.

"Brilliant," said Jamie. It was the first piece of good news he'd had since he'd woken up.

"Let's start tomorrow."

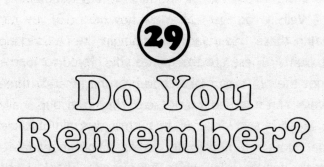

# 29
# Do You Remember?

"Hello, stranger," said the girl, laying down about twenty football magazines and two DVDs for Jamie as she arrived. "Long time no see."

"Jack!" said, Jamie, his face immediately brightening. "So good to see you."

"Likewise," smiled Jack. She had been so badly affected by the news when it had come through that she had immediately tried to book a flight to Spain. Had it not been for the fact that only family were allowed to see Jamie while he was unconscious, she would have been by his side the entire time. "So how are you? Your mum told me it's complicated?"

"Kind of," said Jamie. "Memory-wise, I can remember everything now, except what happened in Barcelona.

And football-wise, we don't know yet. They reckon the head injury has affected my coordination, which explains why I'm walking like I'm drunk. I'm going to work with Archie over here until I'm ready to go back."

"Well, if you want to know how you did, you can watch these," said Jack, holding up the DVDs she'd brought. "These are the games you played for Barça. I got the office to make copies for me. You did well, Jamie. You smashed it over there. They love you!"

"Really?" said Jamie. His huge smile was unmistakable. The colour returned to his cheeks. "You know what? I really needed someone to tell me that. Thanks, Jack, you're a great mate."

There was a short silence.

"Can I ask you a question, Jamie?" said Jack.

"Course you can."

"Is *everything* that happened in Barcelona a complete blank for you? Can you remember any of the conversations that you had with … people out there?"

"Nope. Not a thing. It's a complete blank. It's like those whole couple of months have been erased. It's mental. To think I've played for the best club in the world and I can't remember any of it. That's why it's lucky you brought me those DVDs."

Jamie looked at Jack. Her face seemed to have changed.

"You OK, Jack?"

"Yeah, it's just… I'm fine. Look, I've got to coach my girls' team tonight and I've got loads to do at the office. I'll catch up with you later, OK?"

"OK, mate," smiled Jamie. "Thanks for coming."

# A Hawk's Eye

## *Saturday 6 October*

"Was it as bad as it sounded on the radio?" asked Jamie as he and Archie started doing some light stretches in Jamie's bedroom before their first session.

Archie had come straight over after Hawkstone's humiliating third straight defeat at home in the league.

"Worse," said Archie. "I don't know why people are surprised, though. We've sold all our best players to pay the bills. Don't tell Jack this, but the players haven't been paid for three weeks. No wonder they're not putting it in on the pitch. They're even offering odds on us becoming the first team to get relegated the season after winning the Premier League. Anyway, don't get me started on that, you'll just depress me! Right, to begin with I just want to see how your coordination is."

He produced a small brown sponge ball and held it in the air for Jamie to see.

"Try catching this," he said, tossing it into the air.

Jamie watched the ball spin and spiral into the air. He tried to engage his brain. The part that analysed the flight and pace of the ball and told his body what to do.

But he couldn't find the switch to turn it on.

Jamie flung out his hands but could only watch as it fell past his clutches on to his bedroom floor.

"Ha!" Jamie laughed. "Wow! Don't know what happened there! Bit of a muck up!"

"Don't worry," Archie reassured him. "I spoke to a few doctors yesterday. They all say it'll take time. Do you think you can throw the ball back to me?"

"Of course!" said Jamie. "I'm a footballer, remember, not a complete malco!"

Jamie reached down to pick up the ball and felt his head tumble into a well of dizziness. He almost fell over as he grasped for the ball, having to cling on to the side of his bed to maintain his balance.

"You OK?" asked Archie.

Jamie nodded.

"OK, then," said Archie. "I just want you to loop the ball back to me. A light throw, as if you were lobbing it to a young child."

"Cool," replied Jamie, readying himself to apply his

maximum concentration to this next task.

He took a deep breath and threw the ball into the air.

However, instead of producing a soft, sympathetic lob, which was what his mind had asked his body to do, his hand jerked forward involuntarily and tossed the ball directly into his own face.

Jamie collapsed on to the bed. Almost immediately he understood what the doctor had been trying to tell him in Spain. This was not a normal injury. This was not about his playing football again. Right now, it was nowhere near that.

This was about whether his brain could ever recapture control of his body.

# Crowd Pleaser

***Saturday 20 October – two weeks later***

There were five minutes to go until kick-off and, led slowly by Archie Fairclough, Jamie Johnson made his way on to the Hawkstone United pitch for the first time in five months.

He was not here to play, however. Just to show his support for *his* club.

Archie had invited him along, thinking that watching a game live – seeing the action close up – might help Jamie to access his football brain. They had tried to kick a football together for the first time this week but it had gone terribly; Jamie had fallen over twice.

That was when Archie had suggested coming along

to the game.

"It might just make something click," he'd said. "And anyway, the players are all desperate to see you."

Jamie had quickly agreed and had been massively excited about the prospect but, when he heard the PA announcer pipe up just as he was about to take his seat behind the dugout, Jamie knew he'd made an awful mistake.

"Ladies and gentleman." The announcement had come in a loud, booming voice and with far too much drama for Jamie's liking. "If you were watching the match between Barcelona and Real Madrid some four weeks ago, you will no doubt have seen the awful accident involving Jamie Johnson, the hugely popular former Hawkstone United player…"

Suddenly Jamie's face appeared on the big screen and a hush descended on the crowd, followed by the sound of thirty-five thousand people all whispering and gossiping at the same time:

*I thought his head had actually come off.*

*What a tragedy … I hope he's going to be OK.*

*I heard he still can't speak properly.*

*What a player – we could do with him now!*

"…Well, we're very pleased to say that Jamie is recovering well and is back with us for today's game … and we'd like to invite him on to the pitch now to receive your applause!"

A terrific roar reverberated around the ground. Fans stood up and clapped. Fathers put their arms around their sons and pointed proudly in Jamie's direction. *If only they were clapping me scoring a goal,* Jamie thought to himself, *rather than just feeling sorry for me.*

Initially Jamie thought he might be able to get away with just a wave, but the applause was too much. The fans wanted to see him.

So here Jamie was: slowly, painfully, shuffling his way on to the pitch. He could now walk without the crutches but he knew his body well enough to be certain that he couldn't clap and walk at the same time, so he had to wait until he'd made his way fully into the centre circle before he could in any way acknowledge the stunning ovation he was receiving.

The last time he had stood on this pitch, he had been parading the Premier League trophy in front of the fans – sprinting around the ground in pure joy.

Today was different. Jamie knew he was collecting the fans' sympathy rather than their admiration.

Finally, he raised his hands and clapped the fans back, trying to be the returning hero they so wanted him to be.

But for Jamie, this was not a thrill. It was torture. This pitch, this canvas of dreams, was the only place he wanted to be. But not like this. Not as a shadow of himself.

Within five minutes of the game starting, he'd gone, slipping quietly out of one of the exits and making his way home.

Jamie understood why Archie had thought that watching the game might help. The hope was that, as Jamie watched the action, his brain would finally click into gear and neatly present Jamie with all the abilities that he'd lost.

But life wasn't that perfect. Instead, it had felt more like a form of torment: Jamie being forced to watch other people do what he so desperately wanted to do.

He'd had to walk home from the ground because he couldn't even run properly. It was as though his body would not receive his brain's commands and there was nothing he could do to change it.

"You're early!" Jamie's mum said as he trudged through the brand-new door of their brand-new house, slamming it shut behind him. "How did it go? Any good kicks?"

"I hate myself," was all he could offer, before dragging himself upstairs to his room.

Slowly but surely, not being able to play football was killing Jamie.

# 32
# A Keeper Saved

## Wednesday 24 October

"So tell me about some of the stuff we got up to," said Jamie.

Even though he and Archie had started to make some progress with throwing and catching a ball, Jamie had still been in something of a depression for the last few days. But when Jack reminded him that Stonefish had been living with him out in Barcelona, he knew there would be some funny stories to cheer him up.

"Ah! Where do I start?" said Stonefish. He was still living in Jamie's apartment out in Spain, waiting for him to come back. "Well, a couple of days after I arrived, you fell asleep on the beach so I put factor 40 suncream lotion on your forehead spelling the word BUM but left the rest of you to burn. So, when you woke up, you were bright red all over, except for the word BUM, which was written in big white letters on your head!"

"NOOOO!" laughed Jamie. "You've got to be kidding me! What did the Barça players say?"

"They were just happy to learn a new, rude word in English!"

"So did I get you back, Stonefish? Please tell me I got you back!"

"Oh, you got me back all right. One night, we decided to go out to the disco and when we were getting ready, without me knowing it, you replaced the shampoo in my bathroom with hair remover. So I wash my hair with this stuff and by the time we get to the disco, I am chatting to this girl and my hair is falling out in clumps. I'm literally going bald in front of her eyes!"

"You serious?! Well, I guess we're even then!"

"Oh, there's loads more, Jamie, I'm just getting started. Wait till you hear about the rollercoaster story! I ended up being sick and the people behind me had their mouths open!"

Jamie and Allie both cracked up for a good two minutes. "So we had a good time, you and me?" asked Jamie between the laughter.

"The best," said Stonefish. "I was going nowhere

before you asked me to come out to join you. I'd retired. My dad had died and I wasn't looking after myself. I honestly don't know what would have happened to me if you hadn't got in contact..."

Suddenly the line went quiet.

"Stonefish?" said Jamie. "Stonefish, are you crying?"

"No," came the response between the sniffles.

"Come on, Stonefish," laughed Jamie. "I called you so you could cheer me up and now you're the one crying!"

"I can't help it, man," said the big goalkeeper through his sobs. "You saved me, man. I'll never forget that."

# ㉝
# The Deal

Jamie had spent so long on the phone trying to get Stonefish to stop crying that he hadn't even heard Archie arrive for today's fitness session.

He was halfway down the stairs when he heard the conversation that was taking place in the kitchen.

Something about the tone of the voices made Jamie stop, slowly crouch down and continue to listen.

"What do you mean, they don't have to pay him anything?" Jamie's mum was saying.

"They don't owe Jamie anything," said Archie flatly. "He's on a pay-as-you-play deal. If he's not fit enough to play, he doesn't get paid."

"Now, hang on a minute," Jeremy interjected. "I read through that contract several times. There was never any mention of 'pay-as-you-play'. I would never have allowed him to sign something like that. This is ludicrous. Let me speak to Barcelona."

"The contract you saw wasn't the one that Jamie signed," revealed Archie. "Turns out he failed the medical because of his knee but, instead of letting the deal break down, he told Godal that he would sign for them on a pay-as-you-play deal... I guess that was how much Jamie wanted to sign for Barcelona. Apparently it was his suggest—"

And then, as Jamie appeared in the room, Archie's voice tailed off.

"I don't remember doing it," said Jamie, "but you know how desperate I was to play for Barcelona. I would have done anything to make it happen. And ... it sounds like I did."

"I'm so sorry, Karen," Archie offered, seeing Jamie's mum slump into a chair as she took in the news that Jamie had been left with nothing. "I've been in football for fifty years and I can honestly tell you that your son is the most naturally gifted player that I have ever had the privilege of working with. I don't mind saying that in front of him because he knows what I think of him anyway. I have a theory that the way people play football tells you a lot about their character. Not only is your son one of the best players I have ever seen, he's also the bravest."

"So what happens now?" asked Jamie's mum.

"I can only tell you one thing for sure," stated Archie. "We will not give up on his football career without one hell of a fight."

## 34
# Surprise Offer

### *Monday 29 October*

Dillon Simmonds. Dillon Jay Simmonds.

Of all the people who had wished Jamie a speedy recovery or started being nice to him, this was not one he was expecting.

Over the last few weeks, Jamie had been stunned by the amount of people who had got in touch or wished him well. Señor Godal called him every few days, always with the same message: there is no rush, we are here waiting for you. But in some ways, it was the letter that Jamie had received from Fernando Nemisar, the Real Madrid manager, that had made more of an impression – just because it was so unexpected.

The letter had arrived very quickly after the injury, on the fantastic-looking headed notepaper of Real Madrid, and Nemisar had even taken the time to hand-write it. In the letter he'd said how sorry he was about what had happened and that his club and all its supporters wished Jamie a full and speedy recovery.

Jamie still couldn't remember the accident or ever having come into contact with Nemisar personally, but he was fully aware of his reputation as being a man with only ego and no heart. His letter proved that the reality was different to the reputation.

First Nemisar and now Dillon Simmonds. Jamie's condition was affecting other people almost as much as him.

Since the first time they had met, aged eleven – when Dillon had asked Jamie to help him find a nonexistent contact lens on the ground and then promptly kneed Jamie up the bum – their relationship had been a negative one.

All the way through school, Dillon had made Jamie's life a misery. "Ginge", "Muppet", "Egg", and "Worm" were among the nicest names that Dillon had given to Jamie. Meanwhile, the fact that he had always been twice Jamie's size had also given him a considerable advantage whenever Jamie had cracked and challenged Dillon to a fight.

Which made it all the more surprising that, today, Dillon was being mysteriously, ridiculously, unfathomably nice.

They had run into each other at the local gym – Archie had told Jamie that he should lift some weights to build up his muscle strength – and Dillon had been nothing but smiles.

"I've given up football," Dillon announced, entirely unprompted, as he yanked hard on the rowing machine. He'd turned pro at the same time as Jamie but had been nowhere near Jamie's league.

"Right," replied Jamie, unsure whether he was supposed to act as if he cared.

"It was going nowhere, so I'm a builder now," Dillon continued, unperturbed. "I've set up my own company and it's going seriously well. Cash, mate. Serious amounts of cash. And with all the heavy lifting, you get these!"

Dillon pulled up a sleeve of his T-shirt to reveal a huge, bulging bicep.

"It was Jack Marshall who helped me, actually. She was wicked. I went to see her 'cos she's like the cleverest girl from our school and I just asked for her help. I was like: 'Football's giving me no money and I've got both me and Robbie to worry about, what should I do?' And she sat there with me for a couple of hours asking what

I was interested in, what I was good at, and she said 'cos I liked working with my hands I should think about building. Then she introduced me to her dad, who owns some houses he rents out, and it all kind of went from there.

"Top girl, she is. And it doesn't hurt that she's as hot as anything either. It ought to be illegal how good-looking that girl is! What's happening with you and her, anyway? You're always together, but—"

"We're friends," said Jamie sharply. This was none of Dillon's business. And the mention of Jack's name also pricked Jamie's feelings. She hadn't been round in a while and Jamie couldn't quite work out why.

"Fine, you don't want to talk about it. I get it," smiled Dillon, with a hint of his old schoolboy malice. "Well, anyway, I owe her one and, seeing as you and her are 'friends', I thought I would offer you a hand."

Dillon suddenly turned and looked at Jamie. His expression was so overly serious it was as if he were reading the news on TV.

"So, if you wanted to earn a bit of dosh, you should come and work for me. I can always do with an extra pair of hands."

Jamie looked at Dillon. He might have taken a potentially life-threatening blow to the head but he was not a charity case.

"Thanks for the offer, but if I need your help, I'll ask for it," snapped Jamie, allowing the weights to clank back down. "Remember, *mate – I'm* a footballer, not a builder."

It had been a good line, which had managed to shut Dillon up.

Jamie just hoped it was still true.

# Relative Values

## *Wednesday 14 November – two and a half weeks later*

Jamie stood by the window. It was 4.29 p.m. Normally she was like clockwork every Wednesday evening.

Sure enough, just after 4.31 p.m., Jack Marshall rode down the street with her rucksack on her back and her laptop bag slung over her shoulder. She was on her way to coach her girls' football team, and later she would head back to the newspaper office for the night shift.

Jamie watched her go. Just as he did at the same time every Wednesday. When he'd first come home from Spain, Jack had always looked up at his window and waved at him, but she'd stopped doing that now.

Had he done something wrong? He just couldn't work out why she was being so distant. Then again, perhaps she was just busy. While Jamie was still trying to piece his life back together, other people were getting on with theirs.

Jamie turned, opened his wardrobe and started to take off his running clothes. His balance was improving enough now that he could do it standing up.

In fact, the training sessions were starting to get much better. He was now kicking a ball against the wall quite hard, and Archie had even said that Jamie might be able to take part in some light training with the Hawkstone Youth Team in a month or two's time – if Godal agreed.

However, two months seemed a lifetime away, and if there was one quality that Jamie did not possess in abundance, it was patience. He was desperate to play again, desperate to feel like the player he knew he'd been.

As he pulled off his sweaty top, Jamie looked at himself in the mirror and analysed his features. The hair, previously ginger, now a darker auburn – that was from his nan. The lips, nose and chin were from his mum. But the eyes – their shape and their misty blue colour – were they from his dad?

Turning sideways on, Jamie tried a smile and a scowl. And there it was, in the scowl, just a hint, just a shadow of his dad.

Since Jeremy had told him a couple of days ago that his dad was now in prison, Jamie had been doing a lot of thinking about that man, and the role he had played, or rather *not* played, in Jamie's life...

The slamming of a car door outside brought Jamie back to reality. It was his mum. She was arriving back from work and struggling to carry five bags of shopping to the door. It was a dreary afternoon and Jamie could suddenly see the years of work and stress etched into the lines on her face as she struggled through the clawing winds to the front door.

Suddenly, Jamie felt a dagger of guilt cut into him. When he'd become a professional footballer, he'd promised his mum that she could stop work; that he would look after the money from now on. But in signing that stupid contract, he'd left himself with no protection, and she'd had to go back out to find a new job.

A hideous question inserted itself into Jamie's mind. Had he done exactly the same thing as his dad had done all those years before? Had he promised everything and given nothing?

Jamie looked at himself in the mirror one final time.

Who was he?

Was he slowly becoming the one person he could not bear to be?

# The Deep End

## Monday 19 November – two days before the final Champions League Group Games

Jamie still had the number in his Spanish phone, so he dialled it.

It rang five times before he answered it.

"Señor Godal!" said Jamie, his voice thick with excitement and apprehension. "It's Jamie Johnson here... I just wanted to wish you luck for the game against Rosenborg on Wednesday... Yes, I'm starting to feel a lot better now... I think I might be ready to come back. In fact, no. I *am* ready to come back."

Yes, it was wrong. Jamie had only just started kicking

a ball again with Archie and had not yet showed anything like his old prowess.

Yes, it was too soon. The injury itself had been only just under two months ago. Medically speaking – psychologically, even – he was nowhere near ready.

And yes, it was a gamble. But at the same time, it had been a gamble that had got him into this situation in the first place, so it might just be a gamble that was required to get him out of it.

Not that Archie had been happy.

"Are you mad?" he'd responded when Jamie told him. "You realize this is completely the wrong decision?"

But by now, Archie knew Jamie well enough to understand that when he had his heart set on something, there was no way of talking him round. Especially where football was concerned. So, in the end, he had no other choice than to give Jamie a massive bear hug and wish him the best of luck.

Jamie didn't want to get his mum's hopes up, so he told her that he was going to see a doctor down in London and that he might even have to stay overnight.

When the minicab arrived, Jamie headed straight for the airport.

In his bag he had his passport. And his football boots.

# (37)
# Heads Up

Stonefish picked Jamie up from the airport, Jamie's conveniently dipped baseball cap having allowed him to travel pretty much unrecognized.

They headed straight for the training ground.

It was as though Jamie was in some kind of strange trance. As they travelled along the roads of Barcelona on Stonefish's moped, he felt echoes of having been here in a former life, but nothing so clearly defined as could be called a memory.

It was the same when Godal and his Barcelona teammates greeted him. They showed him a warmth and a care that he felt he did not deserve. Jamie knew who these men were – of course he did, they were the most famous football team in the world – and yet he did not know in what way they knew him.

But in a sense, none of this mattered. The only relevant fact was that Jamie was about to play football with them.

As he jogged out on to the pitch, Jamie felt sure that within seconds he'd be able to tell if that spark was still there, if that football brain was still working inside him. If he could produce just one moment of magic today, one glorious glimpse of genius, that would be enough. Enough to show Godal that Jamie Johnson was on his way back. Enough to show that he had a future with Barcelona.

However, Jamie could feel that something was not right almost as soon as Godal blew his whistle to start the practice game. The first time he ran to chase the ball he felt his head banging as his brain seemed to crash against his skull.

After a couple of minutes, Godal interrupted the game to make some small tactical alterations. It was the second that Jamie needed to clear his head, to focus on what he was here to do. He tapped his chest hard, just above his heart, to get the blood pumping.

Godal restarted the game by rolling the ball straight to Jamie. Had he planned this or was it a coincidence? Jamie watched as the small, round object that contained all his dreams spun towards him. It was coming so very fast.

And really, that was the difference. Before, whenever Jamie had played, it had seemed like everything was happening in slow motion in front of him. He could see the tackles coming in and avoid them; he could capture the exact flight of the ball and prepare himself; and he could predict the way in which the game was going to unfold.

But today it was the complete opposite. Everything seemed to be happening way too fast for Jamie to take in. His teammates were shouting for the ball as his opponents closed in. It all happened in a flash. He lost the ball.

And it was not all he'd lost.

There was no pace or power in his legs whatsoever.

The final blow came five minutes later when Jamie jumped to contest a high ball in the air. He managed to win the header, but as soon as he made contact with the ball, it felt as if the lights in his head went out.

Jamie collapsed on the ground, clutching his head.

Seeing everybody crowd around him in concern, he tried to get back up to show them that he was OK, but as soon as he did, he felt wobbly and sick.

Godal caught him just as he was about to fall.

And, for Jamie, the look in his manager's eyes said it all.

# No More Games

## *Wednesday 21 November*

Jamie turned on his phone and searched for his name on the internet to see what people were saying about him.

It had been a constant stream ever since his trip to Barcelona. It made grisly reading.

> **Majorb** So gutted to hear about Jamie. Really feel for him. **#JamieJohnson**

> **HawksFans** Sad news. U can watch him try to train w/ Barça here: http://bit.ly/w26L@m At 6.21, he tries to head the ball and collapses. **#JamieJohnson**

155

**StueyMawhers** Cld be the end for him. He ain't exactly the sharpest tool in the box. If he can't play football, what do you reckon he'll do? **#JamieJohnson**

**LindyMargot** Jamie is my son's favourite footballer. He's in tears now because he's just heard that JJ's career is probably over. How sad! **#JamieJohnson**

**BarçaNews** Godal asked about Johnson's future at press conference. Said: "It does not look good, but it's a decision for Jamie now." **#JamieJohnson**

**XabiDB** I've met Jamie Johnson. Great guy and proud too. Being embarrassed like that will be tearing him up. Needs our support now. **#JamieJohnson**

Jamie put his phone down beside his bed and closed his eyes. It was just his luck that someone had filmed the practice game and put it on the internet.

Now his nightmare had been laid bare for everyone to see.

"Do you want a hug?" asked Jack.

Jamie had completely forgotten she was in the room. This was the first time she'd come to visit him in a week. Something had definitely been different between them since the injury but Jamie could not put his finger on what it was. There seemed to be a distance between them that had never existed before.

Jamie shook his head. He didn't want a hug. Didn't deserve a hug. He wished he could just close up his whole body and hibernate for the rest of his life.

"Jamie," said Jack, her brown eyes misty with concern. "I need to tell you about some conversations we had in Barcelona. It's important … it's about us…"

But Jamie was back on his phone, torturing himself with the ten new messages about him that had appeared in the last two minutes.

"What did you say?" he just about mustered, without ever fully drawing his eyes away from the phone's screen.

"Oh forget it," said Jack, getting up to leave, before adding under her breath, "Just like everything else."

She left before Jamie could see the tear in her eye.

# The Final Whistle

## *Monday 26 November*

It had been the fact that even Archie had not tried to change his mind. That was what had settled it for Jamie.

Jamie had expected Archie to say that he was being stupid; that they should carry on, that they would get there in the end. But Archie hadn't. Just like everyone else, Archie had seen the footage of what had happened when Jamie had tried to head the ball.

So when Jamie told him what he was planning to do, Archie had just looked at him with a face of pure sorrow and nodded his head. The spark of hope had gone from his eyes.

That was the moment that Jamie knew the game was up.

Even then, though, he still hadn't acted on it. For the whole weekend, he'd turned it over again and again in his mind to see if there was another solution.

But there wasn't. This was the only way.

So here Jamie Johnson sat, alone at his desk, composing the most difficult letter he had ever written.

Dear Señor Godal,

Firstly, I want to thank you for everything that you have done for me.

I still can't remember playing for Barça but, in a way, it doesn't matter. To know that I have done it makes me so unbelievably proud. I will always think of Barça as the greatest club in the world.

I haven't watched the accident against Madrid back yet but people have told me what happened. That injury has changed everything.

I'm not the same player any more.

I'm not that Jamie Johnson any more.

Each day I wake up, hoping that this will be the day that it comes back to me. And it never does. And what happened last week proved it to both of us.

Señor Godal. It's time for us to cancel the contract.

It's time to let me go.
Thank you from a person who will always be grateful.
I hope you can forget what happened last week and just remember me as the player you signed. That would make me happy.
Jamie Johnson

# (40) Reaction

## Tuesday 27 November

## Final Whistle for Johnson

Former Hawkstone and Barcelona starlet Jamie Johnson has been forced to retire from the game at the age of nineteen. Following a brave battle to win back his fitness, Johnson finally accepted defeat in a personal message to Barcelona yesterday.

# Football

## Fairclough rues "tragic" news

"I can't quite believe it, to be honest," said Archie Fairclough, Assistant Manager at Hawkstone and one of the biggest influences in Johnson's career. "The boy was an absolute joy to work with and an even greater pleasure to watch. The fans used to tell me that, when he was on the ball, that was the moment that they forgot everything else that was happening in their lives and just revelled in watching a genius do what he did best. I doubt whether we'll see his like again. I guess we were just lucky to see it at all."

## FOOTBALL

## Hawkstone flier calls it a day

The boy who lit the imagination of everyone who saw him play has been unable to fully recover from the serious head injury incurred while playing for Barcelona

---

### Dirty Boots

Muddy boots have been blamed for last nights

Aston

## Barça Pay Tribute

"When he smiles, you smile too," said Brazilian maestro Rodinaldo in a joint statement released by the Barcelona players on the club's website. "He was one of the best people you could find. We have a team full of stars but Jamie seemed to shine with a light of his own."

# Next

Jamie Johnson – The Footballer.

It was the only way he had ever seen himself. Even before it had actually come true.

Jamie had believed it would happen for him from his first days at school. He had believed in his dream even when others had laughed in his face.

Not just the kids but the teachers too.

"How many boys do you think I've seen come through this school saying that they want to be footballers?" Jamie's head teacher, Mr Patten, had once asked him rhetorically. "Thousands, if not tens of thousands... And do you know how many actually did it? Zero. So I suggest that you start thinking of another career, Mr Johnson."

But Jamie had done no such thing. He wasn't interested in what had happened to the other kids who had gone through his school. They were not like him. He was different. He had always known it. And if people wanted to doubt him, Jamie didn't care. Every cackle, every joke at his expense was more motivation for him. More fuel to fire his ambition.

He simply kept believing, kept working, kept focusing on the vision he had in his mind's eye of becoming a professional.

And yet now he was back exactly where Mr Patten had told him he would be: searching for a career other than football.

The question battered his brain with continual menace.

WHAT NOW?

# Building Bridges

*Thursday 24 January – two months later*

"OK – Dig!" shouted Dillon, his huge neck muscles straining under the weight of the earth.

He and Jamie slammed their spades into the near-frozen soil and continued to hollow out the trench. They would probably finish the digging by the end of the night, which would mean when they arrived tomorrow they could get on with the fun bit.

Building.

It still amazed Jamie that this was where he had ended up. It had certainly not been his first idea. In fact, it had been somewhere near his last.

First off, he'd accepted Archie's invitation to do some coaching with the younger Academy players at Hawkstone. However, the youngsters quickly became obsessed with trying to get Jamie to demonstrate his skills, which, of course, was the one thing he was now unable to do. So that lasted about two weeks.

Then there had been the ill-fated attempt to become a football pundit on TV. Jamie had been really excited when the television company had called asking him to be their studio guest to analyse a big Hawkstone game. It was a great opportunity for him and the money was good too.

At half-time, the presenter had turned to Jamie and asked him how Glenn Richardson had managed to put the ball through the keeper's legs from such an acute angle. It was a straightforward question which required only a simple answer. And yet that was the moment that Jamie's mind had chosen to go completely blank. All he'd been able to think about was the fact that three cameras were pointing directly at him and millions of people were watching at home. Weird thoughts had started to enter his brain: what if he burped ... or farted ... what would happen if he swore right now on national television?

The questions paralysed his mind. He'd opened his mouth to say something but no words had come out.

He and the presenter just sat there, staring at each other in silence, until finally the director went to the adverts.

In the end, the television company had "invited" Jamie to go home during the second half and released a statement saying that Jamie had been suffering from an illness on the day. Unsurprisingly, that was his one and only foray into the world of TV.

The situation regarding Jamie's future appeared to be so bleak that when, one night, Jamie had sat at the dinner table with his mum and Jeremy to discuss what he could do next, it seemed as if he had completely run out of options.

All except one…

Dillon had opened his front door with a big, friendly smile which had immediately put Jamie at ease. It had been a big deal for Jamie to go over there that night. He'd had to swallow a massive amount of pride to even consider asking Dillon for help, but Dillon had made it easy for him.

He'd asked his brother, Robbie, to make himself scarce and he and Jamie had sat and talked. They talked as they had never talked before. And, in fact, it was Dillon who had started it.

"I was bad, wasn't I?" he said. "At school, I mean. I

remember some of the stuff I said and did. I remember putting old Uriah Snodgrass's head down the toilet. I remember smashing a stink bomb on Doctor Hardy's overcoat. I remember weeing on Miss Prescott's car… And … I remember some of the things I did to you."

Both their minds flashed back to those days at school. Dillon had been a walking, living nightmare for Jamie.

"Why did you do it?" Jamie asked.

"I don't know," answered Dillon. "Maybe I was jealous of how good you were at football… Maybe it was my dad and the way he used to … be with me…"

Jamie nodded. He remembered the time he once saw Dillon's dad hit him after Dillon had lost a football game.

"But maybe that's just the way I was. Angry. And … I'm sorry."

The words seemed to produce an effect on Jamie. Something similar to relief. They didn't take away the suffering that Dillon had caused. Nothing could do that. Those sick feelings of apprehension that he'd had to deal with every day on the way into school, wondering what Dillon had in store for him when he arrived. Those lame excuses that he'd had to offer to his mum for the marks on his face when, clearly, he hadn't "walked into a door". Those were all memories that would never leave him.

But it was time for both of them to move on. To look to the future.

"Dillon," Jamie began. "Remember what you said when I saw you in the gym? I think I'd like to take you up on that offer you made me…"

# New Beginnings

## *Friday 1 February*

Betsy. That was her name.

And even though she was probably even older than Jamie, he still loved her.

And so did Dillon. Even more than Jamie.

He adored Betsy. Probably would have married her if he could.

Never has a boy had such deep affection for a van.

Dillon hooted Betsy's horn outside Jamie's house at eight thirty every morning and off they went to work.

Digging, building, plastering... Together they worked tirelessly every day. But they almost didn't notice. Because, while they laboured, they were having fun.

Not only did they get to listen to music and sing along to all the songs, they also got to talk endlessly about Hawkstone's mad season and how, despite fighting relegation in the league, they were somehow still striving on in the Champions League. And all the while, they were outside doing exercise. Finally, Jamie had found a job – other than football – to which he was suited.

And the more they worked together, the more it became apparent how much Dillon and Jamie had in common. Neither of them had been much good at schoolwork, but they were both hard workers who took satisfaction from actually producing something with their hands. When they looked at a wall they had built at the end of the day, they truly felt proud of themselves.

And as the cement walls were going up, the emotional ones were coming down. Jamie even found himself talking about his dad to Dillon. How he wished he'd been able to have a relationship with him, how he envied the sons who were close to their dads.

One day, Jamie even told Dillon about Jack. About how their relationship seemed to be different since the injury and about how he hoped that they would soon be able to get back to becoming as close friends as they had been before.

It was only when Jamie leapt into Betsy one morning

that he realized he'd stopped hoping for something else.

When had it been that he had actually stopped? About a week ago? Maybe even longer.

For weeks after his injury, Jamie had gone to sleep each night praying that his football skills would come back to him.

He had developed a kind of mantra – "Please let me find my talent again, please let me have my skills back, please let me play again." And he would repeat those words over and over hundreds of times until unconsciousness claimed him.

Then each morning, he would wake up with a mixture of hope and desperation – would this finally be that special day? He would pick up a ball and try to juggle with it. But it would be no use. Nothing had changed.

His football skills were like bright silver fish in a black pond. Sometimes, just for a second, they looked as if they might swim to the surface to come back to Jamie, but the more he tried to grasp for them, the faster they disappeared.

And yet these last few days and weeks building with Dillon had shown Jamie that there was life after football. And a good life too. And so Jamie had stopped praying for the existence he'd used to know. Instead something else had happened. He had become thankful. How many other boys get to play for the football club that they love?

Recently, he'd watched the video recording that his granddad, Mike, had made of the first day Jamie had ever stepped out in front of the Hawkstone fans as an eleven-year-old mascot and wowed them with his overhead kick. How they had clapped. How the electricity of excitement had ripped around the ground. "We've got one," the experienced fans had celebrated. "That boy is a bit special – keep an eye on him!" And how right they had been.

Jamie Johnson was already in the folklore of Hawkstone United. He'd won the Premier League and he'd played in a World Cup. He'd even played for Barcelona. What did he really have to feel annoyed and bitter about? Yes, he would have loved to be able to do it for longer, but he was also immensely grateful for the experiences that he'd had.

Jamie Johnson had done it his way. He'd been the boy who had been born to play.

And play he had.

# (44) Thunderbolt

## Wednesday 13 February

As they had been working on a local house, Jamie happened to be home early.

He was just fixing himself a mug of typical builder's tea when he heard his mum's car pull up outside. He knew Wednesday was her shopping day and she'd have loads of bags to carry so he thought he'd surprise her and help her haul everything in.

Jamie opened the front door. It had been a long, bitingly cold winter, but in the clear bright afternoon light, there was just a hint of spring getting ready to rouse itself.

Jamie took the bags from his mum's hands as they started to make their way back to the house. On the other side of the street, Jack Marshall rode past them on her way to do her coaching.

She waved and Jamie waved back with his free hand. But she didn't stop.

Jamie was just pulling the local newspaper out of the letter box when he heard the screams.

A lightning bolt of fear seized him. He knew exactly whose scream it was.

He let the shopping drop to the ground and sprinted up the street and around the corner.

Jack was on the ground, the wheel of her collapsed bike was still spinning and she had a cut on her head that was pouring blood.

"You OK?" asked Jamie. "What happened?"

Jack pointed up the street, where the thief was running away, carrying Jack's laptop bag around his shoulder.

A sensation of pure anger coursed through Jamie. It was a primeval, caveman sense of fury and it told Jamie that no one could lay a finger on Jack and get away with it.

But the mugger *was* getting away.

Instantly Jamie's mind understood what was happening and what he had to do.

He reached for the nearest object to him – an old, hard football, which was lying in the front garden of a nearby house. Taking a millisecond to assess the speed and angle that the mugger was running at, Jamie tossed the ball into the air. Then, with all his rage focused into this one moment, he unleashed a volley of seismically powerful proportions.

The ball shot into the air with speed and unerring accuracy, whistling its way towards its target, connecting directly with the mugger's head, just as he was about to turn the corner of the street and get away for good.

The impact of the strike knocked the robber completely off his feet, sending him scrambling to the ground. And by the time he looked up, Jamie was running straight towards him, closing the distance with each surging stride.

Seeing the frenzied fury in Jamie's face and the builder's biceps which he now possessed, the mugger left the laptop bag in the road and scampered away, leaping over one of the nearest fences to complete his getaway.

"Yeah! You better run, you piece of dirt!" Jamie shouted after him, picking up the laptop bag and dusting it down to make sure the computer was not broken.

Then he went back to check if Jack was OK.

Thankfully she was being comforted and helped to her feet by Jamie's mum.

"I guess you'll be wanting this for work tonight,"

said Jamie, handing Jack back her laptop bag.

"True," said Jack, looking at Jamie in a way she had not done for quite some time. "And I think you've just written my story for me."

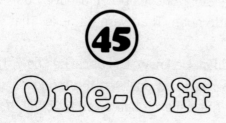

# 45
# One-Off

"Are you thinking what I'm thinking?" said Jack, her eyes sparkling with life.

It was 11.47 p.m. and they were sitting in Jamie's bedroom. Jack had come straight back to Jamie's house after her night shift at the paper. She was now lying on Jamie's bed, with her hands cradling the back of her head.

Jamie was sitting next to his desk, thinking. In fact, he hadn't stopped thinking since that afternoon. Since *that* moment.

"Er, what exactly happened outside today?" asked Jack, putting into words the question that Jamie had silently considered ever since he had struck that football.

"I don't know," he said. "Could have just been a fluke."

"Yeah, right," laughed Jack. "You're about the only person in the world who could have done what you did this afternoon. That wasn't a fluke. That was Jamie Johnson."

He nodded. He knew. Of course he knew. The way in which his brain had analysed the mugger's speed and distance. The instant it had taken his body to adopt the perfect position to execute the volley. And the sweet, colossal power that he had managed to generate into the strike. None of these were matters of chance.

"But what if it just happened because you were … in trouble?" said Jamie. "What if it was just a one-off?"

"Well, that's what we need to find out," smiled Jack, rousing herself from his bed and slipping on her rucksack.

"Where are you going?" asked Jamie.

"I'm *going* to get things ready for tomorrow."

"Tomorrow? What's happening tomorrow?"

Jack looked at Jamie and gave him her huge, big, cheeky grin.

"We're going to do exactly what you just said: find out if it really was a one-off."

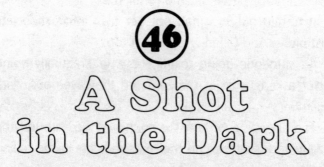

# 46

# A Shot in the Dark

## *Thursday 14 February*

Jack hadn't told Jamie what they were doing. She hadn't even told him where they were going.

All she'd said was to meet her at her house and for him to bring his trainers.

It wasn't until they had almost reached the gates that Jamie twigged.

"Kingfield?!" he said. "What are we doing back at school?"

"Same as we did when we were here – playing football!" said a voice from behind them.

Jamie turned to see Dillon Simmonds grinning at him and Jack.

He was dangling a twinkling set of keys.

"How did you get the keys, Dillon?" asked Jack as she unlocked the doors to the Kingfield School Sports Hall. "In fact, better still, don't tell me!"

It turned out Jack had put her plan into action late last night. And Dillon was in on it too.

"Is someone going to tell me what's actually going on?" asked Jamie as they entered the cavernous, dark chamber.

The air was cool and the sound echoed around the hall as Jack switched on the massive lights in the ceiling to illuminate the giant pitch.

"Right!" said Jack, clapping her hands together and entirely ignoring Jamie's question. "Dillon, you get the balls out of the cupboard, and Jamie, you go for a jog around the pitch; I'm not having you pull any muscles."

"Good," said Jack as Jamie finished his circuit. He was still fit. The building work with Dillon had seen to that. "Now get into the box. Me and Dillon are going to whip over some crosses. All you have to do is volley them into the net."

Although Jack was trying to act casual – as though this wasn't a big deal – she couldn't hide the truth from Jamie. This was another trial. Just like when he'd gone back out to Barcelona. Except at least the cameras weren't present this time.

Without giving Jamie any time to prepare himself, Jack curled in a cross from Jamie's right. It was a quick, powerful centre and the ball raced towards Jamie.

Jamie adjusted his body as quickly as he could and snaked out his foot to fire in a volley.

But he missed the ball completely, kicking only thin air. It was an awful, ugly effort.

Instinctively, Dillon let out a mocking laugh.

"Dillon, you stupid oaf!" admonished Jack. "If you're not going to be supportive, we don't need you."

"Nah, sorry," said Dillon meekly. "It wasn't Jamie I was laughing at; I was thinking about a joke I heard yesterday."

"Good," smiled Jack. "Because you won't be laughing when you see what he does with this one."

And with that, Jack tossed another ball into the air and pelted it straight at Jamie.

As the ball sped towards him, Jamie's eyes zeroed in on it. And then, just as it had done yesterday, his football brain kicked in.

Readjusting his feet, he twisted his body and readied himself for the moment of impact. He calculated the speed and angles perfectly. He was in position for the ball to arrive ... and then when it did, he fairly hammered it into the back of the net. The frame of the goal shuddered with the impact of Jamie's strike.

"Whoa!" shouted Dillon, stunned by the venom of the shot.

"Not bad," was all that Jack said in response.

Jamie nodded back to her. Something very special was happening.

Cross after cross Jamie converted. Some he belted home, some he simply deftly diverted in, but all of them found their way into the back of the net.

After they had sent in about a hundred crosses, Dillon was starting to pant.

"All right," he said, hunching over to catch his breath. "I think we've proved the point. Shall we wrap it up?"

Jack just laughed and shook her head.

"Babe," she said. "We ain't even got started yet."

It was about an hour later that Jack revealed she was ready to try the "final" exercise.

"OK," she said. "This is the one I've been waiting for. We're going to do exactly what we've just been doing but, Dillon, this time I want you to turn the lights off just after I cross the ball; let him see me cross it, but then turn the lights off before the ball gets to him."

"What?" said Jamie. "How am I supposed to kick the ball if I can't see it? That's impossible!"

"Yeah," Jack nodded. "For most people."

*

There was an air of expectation in the hall as Jack lined up to deliver the final cross of the evening in to Jamie. She stepped forward, curved her foot around the ball and chipped it into the air.

As soon as the ball left her foot, Dillon switched off the lights. Darkness.

Except in Jamie's head. In his mind's eye, he could still see the ball coming towards him. He could see its flight and its speed. He could sense exactly the right time for him to strike and ... whoosh; his left foot powered out into the darkness to meet the ball.

At the moment of connection there was barely a sound.

And then the lights were back on. To reveal the ball in the back of the net.

"What the!!!" shouted Jack. "I didn't *actually* believe you could do it, Jamie. It was just an experiment! Do you reckon you could do it again?"

Jamie just smiled.

On a football pitch there wasn't much he couldn't do.

# 47

# Standing Together

As they locked the school gates behind them, a strange feeling washed over Jamie.

"Guys," he said, turning to face both Jack and Dillon. "I ... just want to say thank you."

"What's wrong with you, you softie?" rounded Dillon.

"I'm serious," said Jamie. "My granddad used to say that real friends are the ones who walk in the room when other people walk out. And what you two have—"

"Oh just shake my hand if it'll stop you babbling on," laughed Dillon, stretching out his big bucket of a hand.

Meanwhile, Jack, for once, did not say anything. She simply leaned forward and gave Jamie a hug.

Jamie wrapped his arms around her and breathed in deeply. The scent of her hair filled his nostrils and, as it did so, bright flashes of memories suddenly began to spark in his mind: taking the plane to Spain ... being introduced to the Barcelona fans ... walking out on the balcony to tell Jack how he felt ... working his way into the Barcelona team ... scoring a goal ... becoming a hero....

Suddenly, as all the memories began to collide inside Jamie's head, his legs started to feel weak. He pulled Jack tighter to him. He felt unsteady and needed her support now more than ever. He didn't want to let her go. Ever again.

"Oi, you two," shouted Dillon. "Just 'cos it's Valentine's Day doesn't give you an excuse!"

Jamie and Jack laughed. They were both blushing.

It was amazing. After everything that had happened in their lives, here were Jamie Johnson and Jack Marshall, back at Kingfield School, with Dillon Simmonds standing there teasing them.

Nothing whatsoever had changed.

And yet, at the same time, everything was completely different.

# 48

# Archie

## *Sunday 3 March – two and a half weeks later*

Archie Fairclough had almost cried when Jamie told him.

It was a clear March night. A Sunday. Everyone else was at home, watching TV and relaxing, but Jamie knew where he'd find Archie. The Hawkstone United training ground, preparing for the club's crucial next game.

Jamie had knocked on the door and gone in. Then he'd told Archie everything. The whole story. Every detail of what had happened in the two and a half weeks since, in that moment of alarm, he had picked up that football and ordered his brain to strike it as hard and accurately as possible at the man who had mugged Jack.

He'd also told Archie about all the memories that had been coming back to him, like flashing lights in his head: the day he suggested the pay-as-you-play deal to Godal, the hat-trick he'd scored against Mallorca, and the back-heel goal he'd struck against Madrid. Jamie could remember almost everything now. Everything except for the actual moment he'd suffered the injury.

Finally, Jamie described the secret, night-time sessions that he, Jack and Dillon had been conducting in the Kingfield School Sports Hall. The sessions that had told him he was ready to play football again. Truly ready this time.

Archie had simply sat back in his chair and listened. As Jamie told his mentor the story, Archie's cheeks had filled with colour and his eyes had glistened with emotion.

"I ... I am so happy," he had finally said when Jamie finished the story.

"Me too," smiled Jamie.

"But I don't understand," said Archie, rubbing his thick white beard and shaking his head. "Why didn't you tell me? You could have used our facilities here at Hawkstone. You didn't have to break into the school every night!"

"I wanted to keep it a secret," Jamie replied. "Until I was really sure. I didn't want anyone to know. To get their hopes up. Including me. But now I am sure,

Archie. That's why I'm here."

At that moment, Archie had very nearly started crying again. Jamie could see how much Archie cared for him. It was a beautiful feeling to know that someone existed who just wanted to the best for him and it reminded Jamie of his granddad Mike in so many ways.

Finally, Archie composed himself and stood up.

He took out a tissue and gave his reddening nose a massive blow.

"Well," he smiled, picking up the phone. "I guess we'd better arrange a football match for you to play in, hadn't we?"

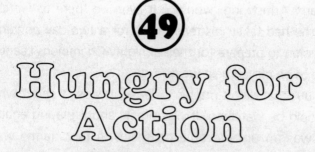

# 49

# Hungry for Action

## *Thursday 7 March*

It was truly disgusting.

The strangest, most bizarre dinner Jamie had ever had in his life.

But no one was saying anything. They were all pretending it was nice.

It would have broken Jeremy's heart to have done anything else.

"There you go, Jacqueline," said Jamie's mum, smiling at their visitor as she filled her glass up to the brim. "It's so nice to see you again."

It was just the four of them and it was a perfect way for Jamie to prepare for his match the next day. Jamie was going to be playing for the Hawkstone reserves against the Academy players, in a special match arranged by Archie Fairclough.

It was just a small game and the Hawkstone manager, Harry Armstrong, would not even be there to watch, as he had taken his team away for a two-day bonding session to prepare for their almighty Champions League tie to be played next week.

But that didn't matter to Jamie. It wasn't about who would be watching. It was simply about playing again. It was an unbelievable prospect. In fact, Jamie was slightly concerned that if he thought about it too much – truly contemplated the fact that he was about to get back out there and play football again – he might physically burst with the excitement.

Which was why a quiet dinner at home with those closest to him was the ideal way for him to relax. Perfect, of course, apart from the food.

"Well?" asked Jeremy expectantly, looking at each of his fellow diners. He was still wearing his favourite lime green apron, which had the words **Dressed to Grill** written on the front. "What do you think? I've used a special type of olives, my own recipe orange sauce and the fish – I went to the market before work this morning to pick that up... What do you think? I didn't go too far with the beetroot and sultanas, did I?"

Both Jack and Jamie used their old-school trick of hiding the fish in the middle of the mashed potato, leaving it to Jamie's mum to politely say: "Yes, darling, it really is very … unusual!"

A slightly uncomfortable silence followed, with Jamie kicking Jack under the table to try to make her laugh.

"Good," said Jeremy, suddenly standing up and speaking in a very posh voice. "I should like to propose a toast."

And then he raised his glass and straightened his back.

"To Jamie," he said, smiling at his stepson. "Good luck for tomorrow. Go for your goals."

Almost without thinking, Jack, Karen and Jamie all nodded their heads and repeated the words back to Jeremy.

"Go for your goals."

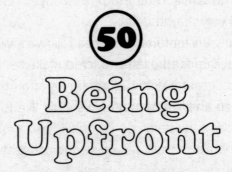

# 50
# Being
# Upfront

## Friday 8 March – the Special Friendly Match

There was a distinct feeling of magic in the air as Jamie received possession for the first time. He rolled the ball cheekily under his foot, forward and back. Then he stopped it dead and allowed it to remain there as he leaned his body first to the left and then to the right.

Finally, Jamie put a stop to the tricks and did what he was born to do.

Run with a football.

He touched the ball forward and exploded like a rocket after it. One defender came to close him down; Jamie skipped past him. Another slid across; Jamie hurdled him like an Olympic athlete. Then the final defender charged at him, but Jamie simply knocked the ball between his legs and raced away.

He was in on goal. He had no need to think. His body knew what to do.

Jamie's left foot flew into the ball. As it made contact, it emitted only the softest sound. And yet the power was truly immense.

The football fairly thundered into the back of the net, rocking the frame of the goal to its foundations.

And while Jamie Johnson held his arms aloft on the pitch, Archie Fairclough hurriedly searched through his pockets on the sidelines.

His hands were shaking with excitement as he dialled the number. It rang twelve times before the call was finally answered.

"This better be good, Archie," said an agitated Harry Armstrong. "We're right in the middle of a team-talk. You do remember we've got the most important game in the club's history on Wednesday night?"

"Yes, gaffer, I remember all right," said Archie. His eyes were wild with childlike excitement and his chest heaved with anticipation. "That's why I suggest that you get yourself down to the training ground as quick as you can…"

*

That night, Jamie opened his bedroom window and looked up at the night sky. As he tilted his head back and stared at the stars, he replayed in his mind what had been one of the greatest days of his life.

The football he had played today had been sublime. He knew it. He could feel it.

And it wasn't just what he had done on the pitch. It was the way his body had felt too. It had actually taken him about half an hour to work out what had been different.

He knew something had changed from the way he had played before the injury but he couldn't identify exactly what. It was only when he had completed his sixth long-distance sprint down the line that it finally dawned on him.

The pain in his knee.

It had gone.

Sure enough, no matter how much Jamie had twisted, turned and tested the joint, it stood up to the challenge. It didn't just feel good. It felt sensational. As good as new.

Perhaps it should have come as no real surprise; every doctor that had examined Jamie's knee had told him the exact same thing – it needed at least six months' rest in order for it to heal. And when he did the calculations, Jamie realized that the period he had been out for – the length of time that had passed since that fateful match he had played for Barcelona against Real Madrid – had been five and a half months, almost to the day.

The ticking time bomb had finally been defused.

Breathing in the cool night air, Jamie smiled as he remembered the sight of Harry Amstrong's car speeding into the training ground to catch the last ten minutes of the match he was playing in.

As he had scored his fifth goal of the game, Jamie had turned to see Harry and Archie in deep, animated discussions on the touchline. And then, almost as soon as the match had finished, Archie had marched up to Jamie and wrapped his big, warm arm around his shoulder.

"I've got one question for you, Jamie," he'd said. "Do you want to play for Hawkstone United again?"

It was probably the single most stupid question anyone had ever asked Jamie in his life.

# Back to Real-ity

## Wednesday 13 March – five days later

### Champions League Round of Sixteen Second Leg

---

Hawkstone United v Real Madrid
First Leg Finished 0-0
KICK-OFF 7.45 p.m.

---

*LIVE TV STUDIO COVERAGE*
*Presenter: Good evening and welcome to what is certain to be a night of pure drama here in Hawkstone. Quite simply, Hawkstone United must win this match against Real Madrid to prevent the club from going bust... I've literally just been handed the team news, and taking a huge gamble tonight is the Hawks boss, Harry*

*Armstrong, who has selected JAMIE JOHNSON to start this tie... Johnson, who, it has been revealed, has been training secretly with Hawkstone since last Friday, has apparently showed such scintillating form in practice that Armstrong believes he has no choice other than to play the little genius... And yet, at the same time, questions remain about whether it can ever be sensible for the nineteen-year-old, who has only just returned from a major head injury, to ever take part in top-level football again....*

As Jamie breathed in the familiar smell of a football changing room, he smiled to himself. He was back home.

Barcelona had been fantastic. Although they still held his registration as a player – they had never cancelled the contract just in case Jamie *did* ever come back – they had agreed to loan him to Hawkstone United, who had made a special request to Barcelona in light of their financial difficulties.

Jamie sat down and looked at the Hawkstone United kit next to him. He, like everyone else in the city, knew that Hawkstone United was now on a life-support machine. That support was the Champions League. If they went out tonight, the machine would be switched off and the club would die. A one hundred and twenty-seven year existence would end. But if they could progress into the quarter-finals of the competition, the money it would generate would be enough to keep the club afloat until at least the end of the season.

It was a simple equation: win and survive or lose and die.

The only thing standing in their way was a certain football club called Real Madrid.

# 52
# Ready for Battle

With ten minutes to go until the game kicked off, Harry Armstrong walked into the Hawkstone dressing room and looked around.

Jamie could already feel the hairs on the back of his neck begin to stand up. Armstrong was a general about to send his troops into battle. Before that, he had one final message for his men.

"I don't have to tell you how big this game is for the club," he said. "I want you to put all of that other stuff out of your mind and just take a look at this dressing room...

"Look around you," he said, each word laced with meaning. "You are a team. And you should be proud to walk out there tonight with these men on your side.

I look at each one of you and I wouldn't swap you for any other player in the world... If I were facing the biggest challenge of my life, I would want *you* alongside me in the trenches," he said, pointing to his big goalkeeper. "And *you*, and *you*..."

Harry Armstrong went around the whole team before he finally pointed at Jamie.

"And you," he said to Jamie.

Despite everything Jamie had been through, Harry didn't single him out. He didn't make any special reference to him. He just treated Jamie like any other member of the team.

And Jamie liked that.

It was all he had ever wanted to be. A member of the team.

Jamie Johnson strode down the tunnel, up towards the light of the pitch ahead. The clicking of the studs matched the rhythm of his beating heart.

And then, as he made his way out on to the pitch, the music started. The same music that had set the adrenaline pulsing through Jamie when he'd watched Champions League games on TV as a kid.

As he stood shaking hands with the Real Madrid players, humming the music as it blasted out around the Hawkstone ground, Jamie imagined football fans all over the globe getting ready to watch this game with their tea.

Dillon and Robbie would be at home, kicking a ball around, having a little wrestle, making their predictions. Stonefish had already told him he would be tuning in from Spain, tucking into a doubly big bowl of baked beans at the same time.

For a second, Jamie's stomach lurched as he considered his dad watching from prison. And then, almost immediately, he was calmed by the instinctive certainty that, from somewhere, his granddad Mike would be watching over him too. As long as that was the case, Jamie knew he'd be OK.

Slowly but surely, it began to dawn on Jamie: tonight – this match – Hawkstone United v Real Madrid – would be the defining moment of his football career.

# Fluorescent

## *Seven minutes until kick-off*

Jamie broke away from the team photo and sprinted off towards the fans, who roared his name as he raced towards them.

As he got closer to the crowd, he saw a quite beautiful sight. In the top right-hand corner of the stand behind the goal was a group of about four hundred Barcelona fans, all mixing and singing with the Hawkstone fans.

The black and white colours of Hawkstone mingled with the blue and maroon colours of Barcelona. Jamie was so happy that the Barcelona fans were there to support him.

As they cheered, the fans lifted a huge banner above

their heads. Half of it was in Spanish and half of it was in English and, when he saw the words on the banner, a huge smile came across Jamie's face.

There were seven minutes until kick-off. Just enough time to warm up and smash a few balls into the net.

As the PA announcer called out those famous words – "Number eleven … Jamie Johnson!" – Jamie raised his hands above his head to return the applause that was coming his way. He clenched his fist and punched the air. He knew the team needed the fans to be pumped up tonight. And they needed to see that he was back to his best.

Jamie knocked the ball out to Glenn Richardson and pointed above his head for where he wanted the ball delivered back to him. It was time for an overhead kick.

As he waited for the inch-perfect pass to be delivered to him, Jamie flicked his eyes at the goal to assess the speed and angle that would be required from his strike.

And it was at that moment that he saw them. All five of them, standing there, behind the goal.

And in an instant, Jamie's world crumbled before him.

They hadn't even been doing anything. Just carrying the stretchers down the touchline to make sure that they were there in case anything happened during the game. But just seeing the paramedics in their fluorescent yellow jackets had suddenly brought the recall crashing back down on Jamie.

Seeing those bright yellow jackets was enough for the memories of that fateful day – the last time he'd played against Madrid – to come tearing back into his mind.

For the very first time since it had happened, Jamie had total recollection of his injury. Launching himself head first to clear the ball … the horrific impact of the Madrid player's boot into his skull … the paramedics rushing on to help him … to assess him… Jamie seeing their jackets and the stretcher and instinctively pushing them away telling them he was fine, despite the booming, pulsating headache like a hammer hacking away at his brain … and then getting to the changing room at half-time … feeling wobbly, dizzy, sick … and then it had gone black.

Jamie now watched the paramedics walking down the tunnel, readying themselves for the game. Instantly, he felt the blood drain from his body. His excitement faded into fear. His confidence dissolved into distress.

"Jamie!" hollered Glenn Richardson from the sideline. "Here you go!"

The crowd cheered as Richardson drifted over a ˜rgeous little dink of a cross to where Jamie was standing. All around fans got up to witness Jamie's overhead kick. The final signal of his return.

But Jamie was rooted to the spot. Paralysed by the memories that had just returned to haunt him.

The ball simply hit him on the shoulder and bobbled away behind the goal.

A murmur of concern raced around the ground.

"Is he OK?"

"His face looks blank."

"He's got a problem."

"Where's he going?"

Jamie Johnson was walking off the pitch.

# No Going Back

"It's all coming back, like lightning bolt flashes in my head!" stammered Jamie.

His heart was beating like a drum and he was breathing so fast he felt as if he was about to have a panic attack.

"I can remember my injury for the first time, how it all happened, and ... I'm worried, Jack. I mean, the doctors have said I'm fine but how do they know what can happen in the game? Anything can happen out there. What if exactly the same thing happens?"

"Jamie," said Jack in the most certain, most positive voice she could manage. She was standing in the tunnel waiting to interview Harry Armstrong just before kick-off. "The doctors know what they're doing. Calm down. Everything's going to be OK."

Jamie shook his head. He was in a state of complete frenzy.

"But I haven't even gone for a proper header since I've come back. I've been too scared. What if it happens again? I can't do it—"

Jacqueline Marshall smiled. She had to stop Jamie talking. And she knew the perfect way.

She leaned forward and gave Jamie Johnson a kiss. A real proper one. And as she did so, she could feel his startled, scared body begin to calm.

"Right, enough of this," she said, pulling away. "Now can you please get out there and give us something good to report on?"

Jamie nodded. There was no going back now.

"I'll see you after the match," he said, before walking back down the tunnel towards the pitch.

"Make sure you do," Jack responded. "And remember... It's just a game."

# Injury Time

---

**Hawkstone United 1 - 1 Real Madrid**
Johnson. 22                    Gazzi. 78

---

Tie stands at 1-1 on aggregate.
90 minutes are up.
Injury-time is being played.
If the score remains the same. Madrid go
through on the away goals rule...

Hawkstone had so very nearly done it. Jamie Johnson's sublime first-half chip – which had seemed to kiss the underside of the crossbar on its way into the net – had, for so long, looked as though it might have been enough to send the Premier League side through to the first Champions League quarter-finals in their history.

There had been other chances too. Jamie's stunning wing-play had created countless opportunities for his teammates but, somehow, each of them had been spurned. And then, with just over ten minutes remaining, Gazzi, the Madrid poacher, had latched on to a loose ball in the box, turning it into the net from only six yards out.

It had been a dagger into the ribs of the Hawkstone fans, with the Madrid coach, Fernando Nemisar, running the full length of the touchline and sliding along the grass on his knees to celebrate with the fans.

Although Harry Amstrong had tried to rouse his troops for one final push, there was a sense in which the chance had gone. They had been so close – just minutes away – only for the dream to snatched away at the last moment.

Many of the fans were in tears. And now, with the referee checking his watch, the final whistle loomed. Hawkstone United, this proud club, this institution that meant so much to those who loved it, was about to draw its final breath.

Jamie picked up the ball just inside the Madrid half and tried to go on one final run, but his legs simply refused. Harry Armstrong had kept him on for the entire game. However, these last ten minutes had been too much for Jamie; his body had been out of action for too long. He had nothing left.

He flicked the ball out to Glenn Richardson on the right wing and staggered towards the box. As he took possession of the ball, there was just something about the lightness of Richardson's movement, the ambition in his stride, that brought one final flurry of hope to the Hawkstone fans. As one, they stood up, straining to get a better view of the action.

In a whirl of skill and agility, Richardson beat his man and bent in a cross to the far post.

It was a powerful, deep centre and it was heading for the exact space where Jamie was now arriving.

The ball drifted over the goalkeeper's head. It hit the ground and bounced up.

It was in the air, just five yards out from the goal. Suddenly it was there for the taking. Everything.

Jamie and the last Real Madrid defender began sprinting. They both knew whoever got there first would win the tie for their team.

Jamie powered forward, injecting every last jolt of pace he could conjure into his sprint. But the defender had a two-yard head start; the distance was too short for Jamie to make up the gap. The defender was already launching his boot at the ball to clear it.

Jamie's football brain quickly clicked into action.

It told him that there was now only one way Jamie could reach that ball before the defender cleared it for ever.

He had to go with his head.

He knew he shouldn't. He knew every piece of logic said he should protect himself. He knew the fear in his chest was a warning sign for him to stay on his feet…

But Jamie let his heart rule his head. He let his spirit lead his mind. And as he dived head first into the air, the world seemed to turn in slow motion.

He could see himself from above, diving towards the ball, just as the defender lashed his boot in the exact same direction.

As he glided through the air, Jamie understood that it had all been building up to this moment. Not just the last few months, but his whole life … ever since that day when his granddad had first given him a football. This was what it had all been leading towards…

The ball was on the line.

The defender swung his boot. Jamie Johnson dived forward. The crowd held their breath.

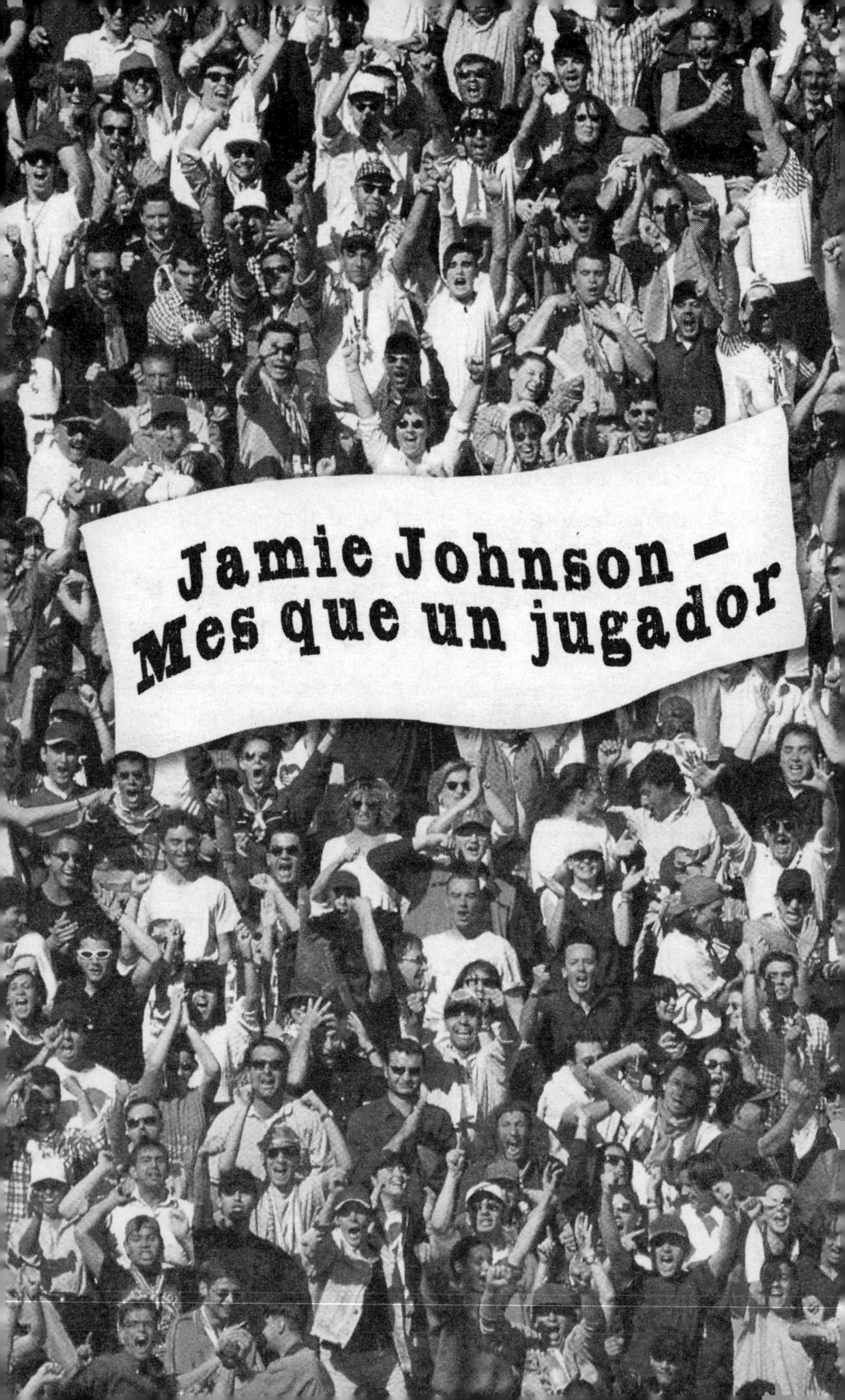
Jamie Johnson –
Mes que un jugador

# Jamie Johnson –
# More than a player

**Want more thrilling footballing action? Catch up on Jamie Johnson's journey to the top.**

"If you like football, this book's for you" – FRANK LAMPARD

It's crunch time for Jamie Johnson

DAN FREEDMAN

"A resounding victory" – THE TELEGRAPH

There's only one Jamie Johnson

DAN FREEDMAN